I0659768

Small Town Reunion

AE Moran

Invisible Publishing Company

Contents

Chapter 1: Jordan

"Welcome home, girlfriend! You're a rock star!" My best friend Anita Seger throws her arms around me, crushes me in a hug, and then pushes me back to hold me at arm's length. "This is going to be so great!"

"Yeah. Great." I glance across the street and grimace at my hometown.

I don't exactly grimace in disgust, but I can think of a lot of places I'd rather be than here.

The town looks a lot smaller than I remember. Low, drab buildings line Main Street. Hardly anybody is moving around even at ten o'clock on a weekday morning. At least there aren't any tumbleweeds rolling down the street, but there might as well be.

There aren't any horses tied up outside the saloon, either, and just as I start to think I made a giant mistake by coming back here, a shiny blue sports car drives past me. It shatters the illusion that Oak Falls is a deserted country ghost town, and a second later, I notice more activity moving around.

More cars drive past us and the town suddenly appears more populated and less deserted. Oak Falls isn't so bad. I'm just not used to it after living in Los Angeles for the last six years.

Anita takes my arm and starts leading me up the sidewalk. "I am so thrilled that you decided to move back here! I've got it all planned out! We can go to the movies on Saturday night and the bowling alley on Fridays. My church group has a social night once a month and...."

"Hold it right there," I interrupt. "I didn't move back to my hometown so you could plan out my entire social schedule for me. I've been living the high life in the city for six years. I came back here to get some peace and quiet."

"Oh, bullshit, Jordan!" She pretends to swat my arm and then goes back to beaming at me. "You can't stand peace and quiet. I don't know why you moved back here, but it definitely wasn't for that. I've known you since kindergarten and I'm your best friend. You'll never convince me that you moved back here for peace and quiet."

I survey the town again and don't answer. She's right. She's my best friend and she really has my number. I didn't move back to Oak Falls for peace and quiet, but I don't want to talk to her about why I did move back.

She doesn't pry. That's why she's my best friend. She pats my arm and tows me forward. "By the way, there's someone who wants to see you. He told me to tell him as soon as you got back to town, so we can go over to the coffee shop now and meet him there."

I skid to a halt in the middle of the sidewalk. "You did NOT set me up with a guy on the very same day that I just got back to town. Please Sweet Jesus tell me you didn't."

"Oh, stop it!" she chides. "I didn't set you up. He just wants to see you."

"Who is it?"

"It's Holden Keller."

My jaw hits the pavement. "You can NOT be serious."

She smirks at my reaction and stops just short of jumping up and down with glee. "Isn't it great! He says he's been your secret admirer for years. He says he was crushing on you hard all the way through high school."

"That's impossible. He was everybody's big football hero and Homecoming King and valedictorian and everything. He didn't even know I existed."

"Oh, he knew you existed! He was madly, heartbreakingly, out of his mind in love with you....and he still is. He says he's been dreaming for years of the day you came back to town, swept into his life, and made his heart complete."

She clasps her hands in front of her chest and breathes these words in dreamy ecstasy. I can't stop gaping at her. She can NOT be talking about the same Holden Keller that I remember from high school.

That guy was drop-dead gorgeous, built like a Greek god, magnetically charismatic, and unbelievably popular. He traveled with a flock of admirers and every girl on campus cried herself to sleep at night because she couldn't have him.

Nerdy art girls like me didn't even bother to fantasize about him because he was so far out of my league that it was never going to happen—ever.

Anita gives me another knowing smirk and pats my arm again. "Anyway, we're meeting him at the coffee shop in ten minutes so we better get over there. You don't want to be late for the rest of your life, do you?"

She tries to pull me forward, but I don't move. "Did you set me up with him? You're trying to hook us up, aren't you? Admit it. You're so transparent, Anita."

"I'm not trying to set you up. I just arranged for you two to meet at the coffee shop. What happens after that is your business."

I finally let her lead me across the street to the Daily Grind Coffee Shop, but I have a very bad feeling about this. Anita's reputation as a matchmaker is the stuff of legend in this town, and by legend, I mean urban nightmare.

She's always setting someone up with someone else and I've already been on the receiving end of several of her disastrous experiments. I don't want to go on another one, especially not with Holden Keller, Esquire.

I have to admit she has my curiosity piqued, though. The Holden Keller I remember was too lofty and untouchable to acknowledge a nobody like me. He would never ask Anita to introduce us on my very first day back in Oak Falls.

Maybe there's some truth to her claim if she's this insistent about introducing me to him. Normally, she'll just come out and say so if she's setting two people up out of the clear blue sky. She wouldn't say he wanted to meet me if he didn't.

I have to find out, even if it turns out to be a dud. Anyway, the Daily Grind was our staple hangout back in high school so I have to visit it anyway just for old times' sake.

I check out the rest of Main Street on our way there. Not much has changed. The same stores line the street with a few new buildings in the background. I catch a glimpse of the elementary school around the corner from City Hall. The movie theater sits across the square with the Veterans Memorial flagpole in the center.

Everything is exactly the way I remember it. Even Anita is the same old Anita. She's been living in Oak Falls ever since I left town. She still works at the coffee shop and probably always will. Only I'm different.

We approach the coffee shop's front doors and I can see through the large plate glass windows that Holden isn't here yet. Anita grins at me when she holds the door for me to enter.

The smell of roasting coffee hits my nostrils and floods me with memories. Anita and I used to hang out here all the time back in high school. It was the place where we made all our plans, organized our social lives, and processed our triumphs and failures. This was also the place where I told her I was going away to college while she stayed behind as a coffee shop waitress.

Not that she cared. She knew long before I told her. I took advanced placement classes in high school while she barely squeaked by with a diploma. She never once considered being anything other than a coffee shop waitress.

She hauls me over to our old booth against one wall. Two sides of the coffee shop cover one corner of an intersection. Both sides look out at the street through big windows so we can see everything going on all over town.

I cast a furtive glance toward the coffee shop's opposite corner. "Oh, my God!" I whisper. "Is that......?"

Anita wrinkles her nose at a guy sitting in a big squishy armchair. "Rafael Mendoza, also known as Rafe the Rake. He's been in Oak Falls ever since you left. I don't think he graduated from high school. He just keeps lurking around. He's never had a job, never had a girlfriend—he never does anything. He just sits around in here every morning messing with his phone."

I steal another glance at Rafe and wind up studying him much more closely. Everyone considered him a player in high school and not the nice kind. He had a terrible reputation as a user among the girls and a fighter among the boys.

He sits with his scuffed tennis shoes propped on the coffee table in front of him. He wears faded jeans, an old t-shirt with holes in it, and his beaten leather jacket looks like he got it out of a secondhand-store dumpster.

His straight dark hair is longer than I remember it. It drapes to his shoulders and the fingers holding his phone look like they have dirt under the fingernails. He looks like the kind of guy that has never had a job, never had a girlfriend, and hangs out in coffee shops every day with nothing else to do in life.

"Do you remember what he was like in high school?" Anita whispers. "He ran with the druggie crowd and then he disappeared at the very end of senior year. We all thought he got arrested or maybe overdosed. He probably spent the last six months of high school in a drug rehab or something."

"So why did he come back here? Oak Falls isn't exactly that kind of place. We don't have a drug problem. You'd think he'd go somewhere that he could access it more easily."

She shrugs. "Who knows what's going on with him? His whole family left town. His two brothers both moved away right after high school and I don't even know what happened to his mom. Rafe showed up back in town and lived with his dad for four years until his dad died. Rafe has been living in his dad's old house out in the hills ever since."

"That's weird."

Anita curls her lip at Rafe and groans. "Everything about him is weird. All he ever does is sit in that chair screwing around on his phone. He never talks to anyone or does anything. He's an eyesore on this town."

"You work at this coffee shop," I point out. "Are you telling me you've seen him every morning for all these years and you've never even talked to him?"

"God, no! I don't talk to him! He's a creep."

"Does he ever order anything?"

"Nope. He doesn't drink coffee. He just sits there for hours.... exactly like he's doing now."

We both look across the room at Rafe. He hasn't looked up from his phone even once since we walked in. He shows no sign that he's aware that we're watching him and talking about him. He doesn't acknowledge that both Anita and I went to high school with him.

Who goes to a coffee shop every morning and never orders any coffee? It's bizarre, especially since he's never worked, never had a girlfriend, or shown even the slightest interest in doing anything with his life. He was a problem child at school and he's as much a waste of space now.

"Oh!" Anita grabs my arm and snaps me back to reality. "Here comes Holden!"

Chapter 2: Jordan

The café doors swing open and Holden Keller strides purposefully toward our table. He wears an immaculate blue business suit and his blonde hair doesn't move when he takes each step. He must have plastered it into place with a trainload of gel.

Everything about him looks beyond perfect with not a hair out of place or a speck of dust on his jacket. He cuts across my line of sight when he walks through the door. For a split second, I see both Holden and Rafe in one glance before Holden moves on.

Rafe looks up from his phone at Holden's entrance and watches Holden cross toward our table. The two men pose such a stark contrast to each other that I can't help but remark on the differences between them. They couldn't be more different if they came from different species.

The next second, Holden passes Rafe's chair and Holden's beefy shoulders block my view of Rafe. Holden bursts into a massive, beaming grin and his cheeks color when he sees me. Wow. This guy is just as stunning as I remember.

Anita jumps up at his approach like she's at a job interview or something. She strides toward him holding out her hand and shakes his arm nearly off his shoulder. She even bows her head to him a few times like he's some kind of Japanese diplomat gracing our town with his presence instead of a guy our own age who went to grade school in the same small town that we did.

I'm so surprised by the way she's acting that I sit rooted to my chair. I can't move while I try to decide if I should be jumping up and bowing to Holden, too.

I'm still trying to decide when he comes up to the table and holds out his hand to me. "Jordan—what a pleasure! I've been so anxious to meet you. I couldn't believe it when Anita told me you were coming back to town."

He pivots next to our table and I see that Rafe is still watching us. I can't read his expression, but he seems to have forgotten all about his phone for a minute.

Anita hustles over to my side fluttering around Holden like the social butterfly she is. "Take a seat, Holden. Jordan was just as anxious as you were to get reacquainted.... weren't you, Jordan?"

Holden smiles down at me from directly above, but something in his expression sets my teeth on edge. Is he faking that smile?

Anita nudges me and I jolt out of my trance to realize that Holden is still holding out his hand for me to shake. I shake it and realize a second too late that I'm still sitting down. I didn't stand up to greet him. Was that wrong?

It's too late now because Anita is practically shoving him into the seat opposite me while she remains standing like a damn waiter or something. She is a waitress at this coffee shop, but she isn't working today, so why is she acting so attentive toward Holden? She never acts this way around me.

He answers the question for me when he pulls out a business card and hands it over. "I wanted to give you this. It has my personal phone number on it in case you ever need to reach me. I know we haven't actually gone out yet, but just in case...."

"Go....out?" I repeat. "You.... want to.... go out? As in...for real?"

He bursts out laughing like I made a deliberate joke. "Of course I want to go out. Didn't Anita tell you? I thought that's why I was meeting you here."

"Why—so you could ask me out—or so Anita could ask me out on your behalf?"

He won't stop laughing. I can't tell if he's genuinely delighted by my nonexistent wit or if he's just putting on a show for people who aren't here.

I take advantage of the lull to look down at the card and I get another stab of misgiving about this whole thing. The card reads, *Holden Keller for Oak Falls County Commissioner.*

Holden is running for office. Now I understand why he's so meticulous about his appearance, but that doesn't explain his behavior.

I look back up at him to find him beaming at me with the same huge smile.... but now it definitely looks fake.

"Yes, Jordan," he's saying. "Would you go out with me on Friday night? I never got a chance to get to know you in high school and I would love to rectify that mistake now. I would love to hear all about your success in LA and how you think we can make Oak Falls the best place it can be."

My brain takes a minute to catch up with what he just said. I've never been asked out with a speech that sounded so much like a political campaign pitch. Is he asking me out or is he asking for my vote?

Anita elbows me again and I flounder to come up with an appropriate response. *I'll have to canvas the other suitable candidates,* doesn't quite fit the bill.

"Uh...okay," I stammer. "Friday night sounds great."

"Wonderful!" he gushes. "Do you still live at 296 Saddle Mountain Road?"

"Uh.... yeah. How did you know?"

"Oh, I know all about you!" He gives me a very suggestive, over-the-top smarmy wink. "I practically memorized your schedule in high school and I used to drive by your house just wishing I had the nerve to go ring the doorbell."

Anita bursts out in a very forced laugh and I look up at her trying to figure out what the hell is wrong with her. The whole world seems to have gone temporarily insane.....or maybe just she and Holden have.

I start to turn back to Holden when I see Rafe watching us from his armchair. His eyes give nothing away and he keeps his expression perfectly blank.

One thing I can definitely tell right away, though. If someone in this coffee shop is acting like a weirdo creep, it's Holden.

Chapter 3: Rafe

I look up from my phone and gaze across the wooded valley in front of me. Dense forests cover the chasms as far as the eye can see with jagged granite peaks sticking up in the distance. That sight always relaxes me before I look back down at my phone.

I tap out a few more things when the crunch of gravel makes me look over my shoulder in the other direction. I stiffen and then relax again when a Police cruiser angles into the rest stop where I'm sitting.

The officer behind the wheel squints at me through the windshield and then says something to the passenger at his side before he parks and switches off the motor.

The front passenger door and the rear passenger door both open and two young women get out of the cruiser. I instantly recognize them from the coffee shop this morning and I would have to be blind not to recognize the disgusted sneer the waitress always gives me.

The other one doesn't look happy to see me, either. She whispers to her friend and they both walk out to the overlook where I sit cross-legged on my favorite rock.

The waitress keeps glaring at me while the other one scans the view with a ferocious scowl. Neither of them looks too pleased with the landscape even though it's so beautiful and majestic.

"Are you following me around?" I ask. "I usually have this place all to myself."

"Don't talk to us, creep!" the waitress snaps. "Just stick your nose back in your phone and mind your own business."

"I was minding my own business when you showed up. What's the matter? Are you so badly behaved that you need a Police escort to drive you around town?"

"Shut your mouth, asshole!" the waitress snarls. "Pretend you don't exist which is what you're going to be doing when we get you arrested for harassment."

She storms off to the Police car, climbs into the back seat where she was before, and slams the door extra hard.

The other one stays where she is and doesn't look at either of us. She keeps glaring across the landscape.

She's actually really pretty—or she would be if she smiled once in a while. Her dark-copper hair tumbles in luscious soft curls past her shoulders and her dark eyes flash with hidden light. She might not be smiling, but she has spirit. Anyone can see that.

She's not as curvy as her friend. This one is petite and muscular, but in a trim, sensual way. She isn't as hard and spare as some girls get when they work out a lot.

She wears casual jeans and flat white sneakers with a short denim jacket. I don't see any jewelry. She keeps everything understated in the nicest possible way. I haven't seen a girl this nice-looking in a long time. Not even the perpetual frown on her face can make her look bad.

"Are you sure you don't want to get me arrested for talking to you?" I begin again. "I saw you at the coffee shop this morning. Did you just roll into town?"

She spins around fast and turns her fierce stare at me. "Of course not! I grew up in this town. We went to high school together."

Now it's my turn to frown. "We did?" I shrug. "Okay. If you say so."

She looks away. "You don't remember me, but that's fine. You were too busy getting yourself arrested and thrown in drug rehab back then."

"If that's true, why am I sitting here a free man while you get escorted around town in a Police car?"

She glares at me again and then goes back to looking at the view. "He's my dad. He agreed to drive me up here on his lunch break."

"That officer is your dad?" I check out the Police officer, but he's looking at his phone. He obviously doesn't care that his daughter is talking to such a hardened criminal mastermind.

I give it one more try. At least she's talking to me and not stomping off. "It's a nice view, isn't it? This is my favorite spot in the whole world. I always come up here to do my best thinking."

"I hate this place!" she snarls. "It makes me sick."

"Why did you come up here, then, if you hate it so much? You went to a lot of trouble to get your dad to drive you up here. You could have spared yourself the effort."

"Why are you even talking to me? Anita says you spend every morning in that coffee shop and you've never talked to her once."

"Would you talk to someone who made such nasty faces at you all the time? In all the time I've been going there, she has never once asked me if I wanted to order anything. God only knows why Frankie keeps her employed. She's the worst customer service person I've ever met."

She stares at me with huge eyes. I can't gauge her reaction, but at least she isn't calling me a jerk and an asshole and threatening to get me arrested. That's a step in the right direction.

She tears herself away and goes back to staring at the view. "So why do you hate this place so much?" I ask. "Why did you go out of your way to come to somewhere that makes you sick?"

She doesn't answer right away. I wait, but when she still doesn't say anything, I give up and bend over my phone.

She startles me by pointing down the road toward the end of the rest stop. "I was in a car accident here. I was riding in the passenger seat with my friend and he drove off the road...right over there. His car plunged down the mountain and he got killed. I would have died, too, but someone pulled me out. I don't know who it was. An anonymous person called EMS, and by the time the ambulance got here, I was lying on the side of the road over there. There were drag marks where the person pulled me up the ravine and left me there. The Police never found out who saved my life."

I study the side of her face. Wow. That is one hell of a story. No wonder she hates it here, but that doesn't answer my question. "Why did you come up here, then? I would think you would want to avoid this place."

She shrugs without turning around. "I don't know. I left for college right after high school and I've been gone for six years. I guess I just needed to see it. I don't know why. I didn't think coming back to Oak Falls would be this hard, but I guess I still haven't dealt with it yet. Maybe that's why I left LA to come back here."

"I'm sorry to hear that. That sounds like it must have been hard."

She whirls around and glares at me with all her old ferocity. "What are *you* doing here? Anita says you don't have a job or a girlfriend or any prospects in life. She says you've been lurking around town doing a whole lot of nothing. What's your problem? Don't you have a life? Don't you even want one?"

I have to grin at her. She actually makes me happy when she challenges me like this. She's the first person who's ever really gotten in my face and demanded answers....not like her friend who just hates me on general principle.

"What's so funny?" she snaps. "Do you think being a drag on society is a joke?"

I don't know what to say to her, so I raise my phone and turn it toward her so she can see the screen. Her jaw drops when she sees what I'm working on. "What the....?"

"It's the stock market. I'm trading Exxon at the moment."

Her eye flicks up to the top righthand corner where she can see my balance. I'm operating with a $5 million trading balance right now.

She blinks a few more times and I put my phone down. "I started trading at the end of high school and I've been making a living at it ever since. This is just my operating balance. I have another account with $15 million and I have a real estate portfolio worth $20 million. Is that enough of a life for you?"

She gapes at me with her mouth open and then jolts back to reality. "I'm sorry. I shouldn't have assumed."

"You shouldn't believe everything your friend tells you....and for the record, I had a girlfriend for five years. The relationship just ended last year, so yes, I have prospects in life. I'm not a drag on society as you call it."

She turns away. "Sorry. I feel like shit now."

I stick out my hand to her. "I'm Rafe."

"I know that. We went to high school together, remember?"

"I'm sorry that I don't remember you. What's your name?"

"Jordan," she replies. "Jordan Cruz."

I stick my hand out a little farther. "It's nice to meet you."

She hesitates and frowns at my hand before she finally decides to shake it. "Yeah."

"So what did you do in LA?" I ask.

"I started my own media marketing company. I just sold it a few weeks ago."

"That's cool. You must be really good at it. Do you plan to do something like that here?"

"I don't see how I could." She frowns at me again. "Why are you still in Oak Falls? You could be living anywhere. Anita says you still live in your dad's old house. Why do you keep hanging around?"

"I don't really know. Maybe I don't want to leave *this* place." I look back out at the view. "I love this place. It always calms my mind and makes me happy. I've never wanted to live anywhere else. I just keep staying here for some reason. It just somehow makes sense, I guess."

"Don't you get lonely to have more people in your life? Don't you ever want to get out and see the world?"

"Not really. I have everything I need. It might be nice to have a girlfriend, but other than that, I'm satisfied with what I have."

Just then, the Police car toots its horn. She glances over her shoulder and her father waves her toward the car.

"I better go," she says. "It was nice talking to you. See you later."

She walks off without waiting for me to say anything else. She gets in the car and the officer pulls out onto the road before heading back toward town.

I gaze after them and then out at the view. That was the longest conversation I've had with anyone since I split up with my last girlfriend. No one in Oak Falls has ever asked me so many searching questions about myself.

I miss Jordan now that she's gone. She grilled me on my life in a way that almost makes it seem like she cares.... or maybe she was just curious because her friend filled her head with so many nasty stories about me.

It doesn't matter why she asked. I'm just glad she did. It's nice that someone is at least curious enough to ask. Most people in this town are happy to just let me exist—unlike Anita. She'd be very happy to make sure I don't exist.

I don't expect anything to change if Jordan tells Anita what I said. Anita will keep hating me no matter what. She enjoys it too much.

Chapter 4: Jordan

My mom squeezes my hand and tries to smile, but her smile only shows how nervous she is. That's nothing compared to how I feel. I'm shaking like a leaf and this nightmare hasn't even started yet.

Anita deals with her nerves by completely ignoring both me and my mom. Anita scrolls on her phone and pretends she just landed here from another planet.

I glance around the doctor's office waiting room. I'm getting really sick and tired of doctors' waiting rooms. I've seen way too much of them since the car accident that almost killed me in high school.

I keep hoping this time will be the last time I ever have to go into some doctor's office. I keep praying to High Heaven that this will be the last time I have to get poked and prodded and examined and studied like a damn rat in a lab.

"It will be all right, sweetie," my mom tells me. "Nothing to worry about."

Why am I shaking this hard if there's nothing to worry about? Why does her voice tremble so badly if everything is going to be all right?

Nothing will be all right, but my throat is too dry to say that. I glance around the office fighting the urge to run for the hills, but at that moment, a young woman in medical scrubs comes to the door. "Jordan?"

I launch out of my seat. My mom tries to keep her hold on my hand, but I'm already marching toward the office. I have to get this nightmare over with and get the hell out of here.

Anita can't pretend anymore that I don't exist. She puts her phone away and follows my mom and me into the office. Now none of us can pretend we're here for some harmless reason.

Doctor Patterson is a lot older than I remember. He's been our family doctor since I was born. He swivels his stool away from his desk and smiles up at me. His face shows a lot more wrinkles, but he looks just as kind and caring as ever.

He's the nicest doctor in the world, but I still recoil from him. I don't want to go anywhere near him. I've developed a phobia of all medical personnel, including him.

He stands up and spreads his arms to hug me. "Jordan! What a delight to see you again! You're getting so big!"

I laugh nervously. "Hopefully I'll stop growing soon and everyone can stop saying that."

I gulp down my horror at what I'm about to do and tolerate him hugging me. I even force myself to hug him back. Please Merciful God make this the last doctor's appointment of my life. I can't deal with this.

"Have a seat." He motions me and my mom to the chairs by his desk and turns to a massive tower of folders in front of him. "I've just been reviewing your file....I also have your latest test results from UCLA Medical Center."

"Did you get my email?" I choke.

He smiles at me as kindly as I could possibly hope. "Of course I got it. I wouldn't be reviewing your file if I didn't get it. So let's talk about why you're here. Let's talk about why you need to talk to a backwoods country doctor when you've already consulted with the best surgeons at UCLA."

"Well...." I falter. "I guess the first thing I want to talk about is the blood results I sent you."

"Yes." He flips open one of the top folders. "Everything looks normal in that regard."

"So the accident didn't damage any of my internal organs—none of my reproductive organs? My blood tests are all normal....so I can still have children?"

"Of course. The organ damage from the accident affected your liver, your kidneys, and your pancreas, but your blood work from all of those is normal. You've completely recovered from your injuries and your reproductive system was never affected at all. I don't see that you would have any problem getting pregnant and your scars shouldn't prevent you from carrying a child to term if that's what you want to do."

A heavy silence falls over the office. The elephant in the room just keeps getting bigger and more dangerous by the second. "Well.... about my scars.... which is the other thing I emailed you about. I guess I was just hoping for a second opinion. I don't want to think it's totally hopeless.... not yet. I want to think the rest of my life won't be ruined by a car accident six years ago."

He nods and waves to the exam table. "All right. Let me take a look."

My blood runs cold. Everyone wants to take a look even though my medical file is stacked with pictures of my injuries. I can see the pictures peeking out of the folders.

I drag my sad, sorry ass to the exam table and sit down on it. I can barely breathe when I pull up my shirt and lie back on the table.

I clamp my eyes shut so I won't see his reaction, but not before Anita turns green. Her hand flies to her mouth and she turns away with a disgusted grimace—and this isn't the disgusted grimace she bestows on Rafe when he comes into the Daily Grind every morning.

My mom barely manages to stifle a moan when she sees my stomach. I turn my face away and cringe when Dr. Patterson starts probing his strong, cold fingers into the scars.

I don't have to look to see what they see. I already know what I look like. I have to see myself in the mirror every goddamn day of my life.

Thick gnarled scars crisscross my abdomen, crawl up my ribs, and snake down my thighs where I got thrown out of the car. Just thinking about my scars makes me sick, but having anyone see them is the absolute worst.

"Hmm," Dr. Patterson mutters. "The keloid accumulation of scar tissue seems more advanced than it appears in the pictures."

"That's what the plastic surgeon at UCLA said," I croak. "He said they could continue to get worse.... but he didn't think there was any way to stop that. He said that, if he did the surgery to reduce the scar tissue, the accumulation could just spread to the surgery scars and I would be right back in the same situation."

Dr. Patterson leans back and examines me over his glasses. "That's what I would say, too and he's a certified plastic surgeon specializing in scar reduction. I'd be inclined to take his opinion. I appreciate that you trust me as your family doctor, but I can't really tell you anything different. I'm sorry. I wish I could."

I pinch my lips shut and put my shirt down. I didn't really expect anything different, but hearing him say those words makes it sound so final.

"There must be something we can do," my mom chimes in, but the quivered in her voice only makes me feel worse. "Don't tell us she's going to be like this for the rest of her life.... or maybe even worse."

"It's like I said," Dr. Patterson replies. "You could try it. You could get the surgery, but it would be expensive. I'm sure Jordan looked into the costs before she left LA and she would have to go back there or to some other major metropolitan hospital to get the surgery done—and that's not counting consultations with surgeons and whatnot. It might work in which case you would still have the surgery scars. You would never be totally without scars.... or it might only work temporarily.... or as you say the keloid tissue could come back later. You could wind up having to repeat the surgery throughout your life."

I can barely make myself heard. "So what happens if I do nothing? What if they keep getting bigger and thicker and uglier and I don't do anything to stop it?"

He turns his eyes to me and smiles, but it's the saddest smile I've ever seen. No doctor has ever communicated so much to me without saying a word. I can't stand that and all the anguish that has been building in my heart explodes.

I burst into tears and run from the room.

Chapter 5: Rafe

I almost trip off the curb and I look up from my phone in time to avoid falling flat on my face. I really need to put my phone away when I'm not sitting down somewhere.

I veer to one side and sit down on a bench in the main square of town until I finish my current transaction. I'm a million miles away when a door slams nearby.

I glance up to see a young woman running toward me with her hands over her face. She throws herself onto the bench next to me and bursts into loud sobs.

I frown when I realize it's Jordan, the girl from the overlook. "Are you okay?" I ask. "What's wrong?"

"Leave me alone!" she shrieks without uncovering her face. She turns her back to me and howls into her hands.

I sigh and go back to my phone. I was on this bench first so I don't see any reason to leave. I study the price chart for Maersk-Sealand Shipping Company. The stock is making some pretty bold moves right now so I need to pay attention.

I almost forget that Jordan is there when she sniffs and mumbles, "Sorry. I shouldn't have been rude. I'm just having the worst day of my life."

"Worse than getting in a car accident and almost dying?" I ask.

She explodes in loud sobs. Whoops. That was probably not what I should have said. Oh, well. I go back to my trading when she moans, "Yes! It's worse than getting in a car accident and almost dying!"

"Sorry about that. Is there anything I can do?"

"There's nothing anyone can do!" she yells. "That's the problem! If there was anything to do, I would have done it already."

"Do you want to talk about it?" I ask.

"No!" she snaps. "I never want to talk about it ever again!"

I put my phone down. I'm not getting anything done here anyway. "Look. I know you just rolled into town and everything, but I was wondering if you would have coffee with me."

She whips around fast and glares at me the way she did at the overlook. Her eyes blaze bloodshot-red and she actually looks scary. "I can't go out with you. I'm already going out with someone."

My eyebrows shoot up. "That was fast! Who are you going out with?"

"Holden Keller. He asked Anita to introduce us when I got back to town and he asked me out."

I groan and lift my phone again. "If you seriously want to go out with Holden Keller, go right ahead."

"What's your problem? He's a nice guy."

"Nice?" I sneer. "He's a *nice* guy? Is that all you can say about him?"

"What else is there to say?"

"That he's an intelligent and interesting and insightful and understanding guy. You could say that he's intriguing or creative or helpful or compassionate or that he's doing great things in the world."

"*You* aren't doing great things in the world," she fires back. "You're hanging out in coffee shops and trading the stock market. You aren't helpful or intriguing or insightful or interesting. Why shouldn't I go out with Holden instead of you?"

I burst out laughing. She really does challenge me. "Look. I wasn't asking you to have coffee with me to ask you out on a date or anything. I want to ask you about high school. You said we went to high school together and I want to talk to you about that. Holden couldn't possibly find that threatening, could he?"

She furrows her brow. "What do you want to talk about high school for? You were there."

"Just indulge me.... unless you think I'm too boring or too much of a creep. I would really appreciate it."

"Fine." She turns away and presents her back to me.

"So why did you agree to go out with Holden on your very first day back in town?" I ask. "Are you that desperate?"

"I'm not desperate at all. I'll probably never go out with anyone ever again."

"You'll be going out with Holden....and me."

She snorts. "Like that means something."

"Why are you going out with him if he isn't interesting or intriguing or helpful or insightful or understanding or creative or compassionate?"

She shrugs. "He asked me out. I have nothing else to do. Besides, he made a giant deal about having a crush on me in high school."

"But wasn't he like the biggest football sensation and Homecoming King and all that?"

"Yeah. I didn't think he knew I existed, but he told Anita that he was my secret admirer for years and that he's been counting down the seconds until I moved back to town."

I burst out laughing and she suddenly looks up and grins at me. I can't stop laughing and she finally joins in. Her whole countenance bursts with light. Holy shit, she's stunning when she smiles like that!

She laughs like she knows Holden Keller is a joke even if he is everybody's idea of perfection. Going out with Holden Keller means nothing to her. She doesn't even know why she's doing it.

"So when do you want to have coffee?" she asks.

"When are you seeing Holden?"

"Friday night."

"How about you meet me at the Daily Grind on Sunday morning?"

She frowns again. "Anita doesn't work on Sunday."

"That's why we should go then. Then we won't have her snarling at us while we're trying to talk."

She laughs again. "She really hates you."

"I know, but I have no idea why. Maybe you could enlighten me."

"Do you really care?"

"Not really. I'm just curious since I've never exchanged a single word with her."

"Maybe it's your bad reputation from high school. A lot of people said some pretty nasty things about you back then."

"Well, you can fill me in on Sunday. What do you say? Ten o'clock?"

"All right." She brightens up. She actually looks pleased about going out with me, not indifferent like she is toward Holden. Things are looking up.

She doesn't dwell on whatever it was that made her cry and I don't ask.

At that moment, the same door she came through opens and Anita comes out with a middle-aged woman who looks suspiciously like Jordan. Jordan hops up immediately. "I gotta go. See you on Sunday."

She hustles away. Anita shoots me a few more black looks and moves between me and Jordan like she really needs to protect Jordan from me. Man, that woman can be downright hateful!

I go back to working on my phone, but I can't stop my thoughts from wandering back to Jordan. I would give anything to be a fly on the wall when she goes on her date with Holden Keller. If she's half as insightful and understanding and compassionate and creative and intriguing and interesting as I think she is, she'll see right through him.

Chapter 6: Jordan

I turn from right to left and examine myself in the full-length mirror in my bedroom. I smooth my dress over my stomach to make sure my scars don't bulge through enough to be seen by the untrained eye.

They don't. I look okay. Maybe, just maybe, I'll be able to find someone who will ever want to go out with me even though I look like the Elephant Woman when I take my clothes off.

At least I still look normal from the outside. I don't have to wear a bag over my head, although the scars might spread over the rest of my body. Then I'll have to hide myself to stop people from throwing up when they see me walking down the street.

I hear the car pull into the driveway long before my mom yells up the stairs to me. "Jordan—your ride is here!"

I tear myself away from the mirror. As much as I hate obsessing about my body, obsessing about it has become something of a masochistic addiction of mine. I can't stop dwelling on it. I really just need to accept it and move on instead of hating myself for something that's totally beyond my control.

I grab my coat and handbag, slip my feet into my shoes, and go downstairs. My dad is already on his way to the door to greet Holden.

Holden strides right up to my dad and sticks out his hand. "It's an honor to meet you, Officer Cruz!"

"Just call me Isaac." My dad shakes Holden's hand, but anyone can see that my dad isn't taken in by Holden's over-the-top manner. My dad is way too down-to-earth and he's like a bloodhound whenever someone is lying or being insincere.

Holden bursts into one of his blinding smiles when he sees me coming down the stairs. "Wow! You look stunning! Wait! I need to put on my shades!"

He holds his hand in front of his face like he wants to protect his eyes and then he laughs at his own joke. My dad smiles at him in a condescending way like he's listening to a toddler trying to entertain adults.

I have to smile at my dad's expression and Holden mistakes it for me smiling at him. He holds out his hand to me. "Shall we go? Don't worry, Sir. I'll have her home by ten."

"Take all the time you want, son," my dad replies in his usual even tone.

I cross the hall and kiss my dad on the cheek. "I'll see you later, Dad. I love you."

"Have a good time, sweetie," he tells me.

Holden is still standing there with his hand out like he's Prince Charming about to whisk Cinderella off to the ball. I guess it would be rude to completely diss his hand so I wind up taking it.

His hand feels warm and strong and protective—exactly the way Holden probably wants to portray himself. So why is he taking such an interest in me? I'm really starting to wonder if he had a crush on me at all in high school or if he just made that up to impress Anita.

Anita does have a reputation in town as a matchmaker, although it isn't a very favorable reputation. Maybe Holden planned this whole thing to get Anita to hook him up with me. Who really knows what he's thinking? I'll probably never find out.

He beams at me showing all his perfectly straight, white teeth as he conducts me down the steps to his car. It's a spotless navy-blue BMW coupe that rumbles as it sits idling in my parents' driveway.

My parents live in a big three-story house in the mountains above Oak Falls. It isn't a mansion on the hill. It's more the modern equivalent of a log cabin with an enormous stone fireplace. The BMW doesn't look right so far out in the mountains.

Holden leads me to the passenger door, opens it for me, and squeezes my hand as he supposedly helps me into the seat. Everything he does just comes across as the fakest kind of play-acting. Why am I even going on this date? I should back out now and go back to my room, but I have nothing else to do on a Friday night and no one else to do it with.

My mind flips back to Rafe. He would take me out on a Friday night. Don't ask me how I know this, but even going to a coffee shop with him and talking about our high school days would be a better way to spend a Friday night than play-acting with Holden Keller.

I'm already sitting in his car, though, and it is a really nice car. It vibrates with deep, luscious, pounding thumps. This is easily the sexiest car I've ever ridden in, but the illusion shatters when Holden slips into the driver's seat.

He grins over at me like he knows exactly what this car means. That look makes my stomach turn, but he's already putting the car into gear and rolling out onto the mountain road.

He steers casually down the mountain like he drives out here all the time. I would be very surprised if he ever leaves town considering his clothes, his hair, his car, and his attitude.

Oak Falls is a mountain country community with plenty of redneck conservatives holed up in the hills outside of town. I don't see a guy like Holden representing them as County Commissioner, but I guess anything is possible.

"You look beautiful, by the way," he says on the way.

"Um…. thanks," I reply.

"You were mind-blowingly hot in high school, but I have to say…. you're a dream come true now. I never imagined you would grow up to be such a showstopper."

I don't say anything. What am I supposed to say? I was definitely NOT mind-blowingly hot in high school. That's exactly what I was not.

I hope he doesn't expect me to keep thanking him every time he compliments me. Maybe that's why he's doing it—so I'll feel indebted to him for salvaging what little remains of my self-worth.

Thinking that just makes me angry. I make up my mind to go through with this date just so I can find out what it is he actually wants from me. Why would he go to such lengths to go out with me when I'm obviously not what he wants?

He drives through Oak Falls without stopping. He continues for a long way into the mountains and finally turns off at a castle-like lodge glowing with light. The stone sign out front reads, *Ravenwood Estates*.

"Do you know this place?" Holden asks me with another meaningful smirk. "It's the only five-star restaurant in the whole county."

He pulls his car up to the front steps, opens my door for me, and tosses his keys to the young valet standing there. Holden saunters over to me and cocks his elbow like he's the Duke of Wellington or something.

I stare at him, but he just grins at me like he's really impressing me. I guess I might as well enjoy it while it lasts.

He couldn't be more delighted when I slip my hand into his elbow and we head up the steps. A maître d' in a tux greets us and escorts us to a table in the lodge's downstairs restaurant.

We sit down at a table in the back. A single candle glimmers in the center of the table. I guess this is supposed to be romantic. It would be romantic with just about any other guy on the planet. What in the world was I thinking? If Anita thinks going out with someone is a good idea, it definitely isn't.

I should have remembered that, but I'm already here. No time like the present to break the ice. "So.... you're running for County Commissioner."

He launches into the same oily sales pitch. "Yes! Oak Falls and the surrounding county have been languishing in the late nineteenth century for far too long. We should have high-speed internet at the very least and the county should support business development that brings higher-ticket traffic to the area.... like this place." He nods at the restaurant around us.

"So how's the campaign going?"

He makes a face. "The locals are all too stuck in their ways. They don't see the potential. I do my best to point out that we could be the next tourist destination for wealthy Silicon Valley tech billionaires. We could be the next Northern California coast if we only had the infrastructure to support them. They all want to work remotely and we're too primitive to handle the internet speeds they need to run their businesses. The county should be doing more to woo them out of town to the untapped raw wilderness where they can help us transform Oak Falls into the premier destination it could be."

I listen in rapt fascination. This dude has definitely been drinking way too much of the Kool-Aid. He actually believes the line of hogwash he's trying to sell people. No one in this county will ever buy into his vision of a premium destination with high-speed internet and Silicon Valley tech billionaires transforming Oak Falls into whatever he thinks they should transform it into.

Now I understand his comments at the coffee shop. He wants to turn Oak Falls into LA.... or San Francisco. Good luck with that.

He snaps his fingers at the maître d' and orders a bottle of champagne. Holden rests his elbows on the table and leans toward me in the candlelight. He lowers his voice to a confidential, almost sexual whisper. "So, Jordan.... tell me about the marketing business that you just sold."

"There isn't a lot to tell." I try to keep my tone businesslike. I don't want him turning this into a lover's whisper. "I started doing graphic design and I got picked up as a freelancer by a big company...."

"International Alliance...." he interjects. "That must have been a very lucrative contract."

"It was, but it didn't last long. It did get me some other big clients that led to more big clients and I eventually had to build the company to handle all the additional work."

He narrows his eyes and inhales through flared nostrils. "That is so interesting! You must have scaled your skills and business acumen exponentially to keep up with demand."

"I guess I did. I had to learn fast."

"It would be wonderful if you could transfer some of that expertise to Oak Falls. I would love to talk to you more about bringing your unique brand of media exposure to the County Commissioner's Office."

My jaw drops. "Hold it. Are you saying you asked me out because you want to hire me—like in a professional capacity? Is that why you gave me your business card—because you want me to work for the County Commissioner's Office."

"No! Of course not!" He laughs too loudly. "No, Jordan, I want you to bring your considerable expertise and unique flavor to something much, much more important."

"What is that?" I don't really want to know. I dread hearing his answer.

He leans farther forward and slides his hand across the table to take mine. "I'm talking about my political career, my dear Jordan. You are the first woman I've met with the brains and the business savvy to take the reins on my career and stand by my side as I reach new heights of success and achievement. The County Commissioner's Office is only the first step in a long, fruitful partnership between us. We could even become the First Couple of the United States, but the whole timeline needs delicate handling. What better way to do that than to hammer out a plan now—a plan designed by you and executed by both of us? We could go all the way to the top, you and me."

I gape at him with my jaw on the floor. "The First.... Couple? You want us to be a couple....for political gain?"

"It makes perfect sense! Bill and Hillary—John and Jackie—Ron and Nancy—the road to political success and influence is paved with couples who joined in an alliance of matched skills, abilities, talents, and experiences. We could be like that, but I need the right woman on my arm. I need a woman not only with the looks but the brains and ambition to make it happen. You've already proven yourself, Jordan. You must be very driven if you started your own business like that and Anita told me that you sold it for a nice healthy chunk of change." He smirks and his cheeks color. "You don't have to be modest about it. How much did you really get for it?"

I shrug and look away. "Not that much."

"Oh, come on! I need you! I need everything you can bring to the table—financially, intellectually, emotionally, socially—the whole nine yards! Come on! What do you say? With my looks and your brains, it's a match made in Heaven."

I stare across the table at his beaming face as the truth sinks in. I came on this date to find out what he really wanted and he just told me.

He wants a wife who can be the Hillary to his Bill—the Nancy to his Ron. He wants a woman as ambitious and as driven and as astute as.....well, he isn't any of those things.

Rafe's words come back to me. Holden isn't interesting or intriguing or understanding or insightful or compassionate or intelligent or creative or helpful. He isn't any of the things someone might hope a politician would be.

Holden definitely isn't doing great things in the world. That isn't even part of his political vision. He isn't insightful enough to realize just how revealing his pitch is.

When he listed the assets he wanted each of us to bring to this project, he mentioned his looks and my brains. That's all he has going for him—looks. He definitely has that. I can't deny he has the looks.

That's all he has, though. He wants me to bring everything to the table and the very first thing he mentioned was finances. He wants me to bring the money I made from selling my business.

That means Holden doesn't have money of his own. He has nice suits and a nice car. That's it. He has the image, but he doesn't have funding. He wants me to do that. He wants me to buy my way into the privilege of being the Jackie to his John. Now I really want to puke.

The waiter brings the champagne and I squirm in my chair while Holden pours two glasses. He raises his and clinks it against mine. "Here's to us and our bright future."

I sip my drink and look around the restaurant, and when I do, I feel the thick mass of scar tissue on my stomach. Holden would never accept that. Appearance means everything to him. He wants someone perfect and I'm definitely not that.

Even if he did accept it, he would insist that I keep it hidden. He would never want anyone to find out. He would treat it like the shameful secret it is—the shameful secret I've been treating it as ever since the accident.

I lean back in my chair studying him even more closely, now that I know everything I could possibly want to know about him. He keeps smiling at me. He loves my attention. He thinks I'm fascinated because I'm imagining our glorious future together. He has no idea that someone could have a negative opinion of him.

He has no desire to find out who I really am as a person. He has no desire at all to find out about my struggles or my hidden pain. He says he studied everything about me, but he hasn't mentioned the accident even once. Does he even know that I was in a car accident?

This isn't someone I want to get involved with—not in my personal life and not in my professional life. I want to get as far away from Holden Keller's political career as I can possibly get before the whole thing blows up and destroys my life more than it already has been destroyed. That's the last thing I need.

Chapter 7: Rafe

I get a surge of exhilaration when Jordan walks into the Daily Grind Coffee Shop. She blows my mind when she smiles at me and settles herself on the other side of the table where I'm sitting. She casts a furtive look around and blushes like she's getting away with something by meeting me.

I can't help but grin at her. A girl shouldn't make me this happy. "Thanks for coming," I tell her.

"Let me guess. This is the first time you've ever sat at a table in this place. Admit it."

"You're right. I'm definitely moving up in the world. Just don't tell Anita or I might have to start eating with a knife and fork."

She nods down at the coffee cup in front of me. "You ordered something. That's another first."

"It isn't, actually. I usually order when Frankie is here. We get along pretty well."

Her face drains of all color. "Are you saying you don't order from Anita because.....because you're trying to make a point or something?"

"She makes money on tips. I don't want to reward someone for treating me like shit for six years straight."

Her eyes dart away. "Okay. Let's not spend our whole conversation complaining about Anita. What did you want to talk to me about?"

"High school."

"You mentioned that. What about it?"

"Tell me about what high school was like for you."

"What do you want to know that for? We were nowhere even near being in the same orbit back then. What could my high school experience possibly tell you that you don't already know?"

"All right. Tell me about what high school was like for me."

She furrows her brow at me. "What?"

"Who did I hang out with? What did I do? What did people think of me? You said people said nasty things about me and that's why Anita hates me. What did they say about me? Were their remarks justified or was it all just slanderous rumors? What was I like? All of that."

"What do you want to talk to me about that for? I barely saw you in high school. You know all of that better than I do."

"Actually, I don't. I had a head injury late in senior year and I lost my memory. I didn't get arrested and I wasn't in drug rehab. In fact, the hospital drug-tested me when the paramedics first brought me in and I didn't have any drugs in my system. My dad and my brother both said I never did drugs, so it wasn't that. The problem is that I can't remember anything that happened before the accident. I don't even know what the accident was. I don't remember anything from before about three months afterward....so yeah. I want to know everything that happened while I was in high school. I want to know what kind of person I was before I lost my memory."

She sits rooted to her chair staring at me in dumb shock. I haven't told many people that story and I knew she'd be shocked. I just didn't expect her to be this shocked.

"You okay?" I murmur. "You're the first person I went to high school with that I've been able to talk to about it. The only people

I went to high school with who are still in town won't talk to me at all—like Anita and Holden. Give me a clue. I would really appreciate it."

She shudders and clears her throat. "Sorry. It's just…. I'm sorry. Just give me a minute for my brain to catch up with me."

"Okay." I take a sip of my coffee. "Take all the time you want."

"So…. you don't remember anything—like, nothing?"

"No. I didn't even remember my family. They had to tell me who they were and we had to get to know each other all over again, which was hard because my brothers had both left town by then. I lived with my dad until he died, but that never really got back to normal, either."

"What about your mom?" she asks.

"I have no idea what happened to her. She was gone by the time I came home from the hospital and neither of my brothers or my dad will talk about it. She might be alive out there for all I know. I'll probably never find out."

"That's terrible!" she breathes.

"It's not that big a deal. Anyway, what can you tell me about what I was like in high school? Why does Anita hate me so much?"

"Well…. it's complicated……"

"Why does she assume I was on drugs and that I'm a creep and an asshole? *Was* I a creep and an asshole back then?"

"Let's just say you had a lot of very rough friends. You hung out with a group that was known for getting into trouble. You might not have been on drugs, but they were. They got in a lot of fights. *You* got in a lot of fights. I don't know about the rest, but that much was definitely true."

"Did you see me get in fights?"

"I didn't have to. I saw the other parties after the fact."

I wince. "Okay. That sucks."

She studies me. "It sounds like your whole personality changed when you lost your memory."

"Well, it would have to, wouldn't it? I don't remember whatever it was that made me such an asshole."

She shrugs. "I guess."

"What else? Tell me everything."

"You...." She squirms again. "You had a bad reputation with the girls."

"What do you mean?"

"You had a reputation as a player—a hit-and-run type of guy. You had a reputation as a user and a......" She breaks off.

"Tell me. Please. Don't spare my feelings."

She won't look at me for more than a few seconds. "Let me put it this way. You paying attention to a girl was considered extremely bad luck. You were violent. You had a don't-take-no-for-an-answer type of vibe."

I stare at her feeling sick. "Are you saying I was violent toward girls?"

"Not necessarily. I don't know if you ever were, but the girls had a definite policy that it was better to stay away from you—like, far away. If you paid attention to any girl, all the other girls were like, 'Stay away from him at all costs'. Everybody knew it. It was universal among the girls. That's all I'm saying."

I gulp. I can't think about drinking anything right now. I want to be sick. "But you don't know if it was ever based on anything substantiated? Did you ever find out for certain if I ever really did that?"

"I don't know if you ever like outright attacked any girl or forced yourself on anyone. You were definitely violent with guys and you were definitely a user and a player and an asshole to girls even if you didn't ever actually take it as far as attacking one of them."

I look away. "I better go. Thank you for telling me. That explains a lot."

She shoots out her hand and grabs my wrist. "You don't have to go. I can see that you're different now. I'm sorry I had to be the one to tell you. You don't have to leave."

I sit sideways in my chair staring at the floor. I hate myself.

She waits, and when she speaks again, she almost whispers in a confidential undertone. "Does anyone in town know that you lost your memory? Anita doesn't know, does she? You haven't explained it to anyone."

I shrug at nothing. "A few people know—friends of mine. Frankie knows....and Dr. Patterson, of course. I don't talk to Anita. I don't talk to a lot of people, so I don't see how they could know."

"Thank you for telling me. I'm honored that you would confide in me."

I snort. "Not such an honor. You don't have to stick around if you don't want to. I won't tie you to the chair and force you to talk to me."

Another long silence falls between us. I don't know what to say. I understand now why people like Anita avoid me. I guess I don't resent her for it so much, now that I know the reason why.

"Turn around, Rafe," Jordan finally says. "Turn around and look at me."

I glance over to find her studying me with a pained, sympathetic expression. She's still here. She isn't avoiding me so maybe I'm not a complete waste as a human being.

I swivel around in my chair, but I can't look at her. I stare down into my coffee cup. The thought of drinking it makes me sick.

"Tell me about the accident," she prompts. "What happened?"

"I have no idea," I mumble. "I was found wandering around in a daze. No one knows what happened and I'll probably never find out.

I had blunt-force trauma to the side of my head. No one knows how I got it."

"What was your life like after the accident? You said you had a girlfriend for five years."

"I met her in a rehab facility in Portland. We went through rehab together, and after we got out, I used to drive down there and spend the weekends with her."

"That explains why Anita didn't find out about it. She only works on the weekdays and she says you never missed a single morning since high school."

"I'm getting really sick of Anita doxing my whereabouts to the whole damn internet." I realize a second later how rude that sounded and I glance at her. "Sorry."

"It's all right. I'll try to stop talking about her."

"I think I know enough about what I was like in high school now. You don't have to stay here talking to me anymore if you don't want to."

"Why don't we talk about something else, then? I don't feel right about leaving when you're obviously so upset about this. I didn't come here to ruin your whole day."

I can't stop shifting in my seat. I don't know how to continue the conversation with this bomb in my lap. "Tell me about what high school was like for you."

"High school was great for me right up until the accident. After that, it sucked. The accident destroyed my whole life."

"You said the driver of the car was a guy. Was he your boyfriend?"

I know right away that I hit a nerve. She looks down at the table and doesn't answer. Her face goes blank and all the light drains out of her eyes. She looks beyond devastated. That accident really must have knocked her down hard. I can understand that.

"Anyway," she mumbles in a flat, dead tone, "I was already planning to leave for college, so leaving Oak Falls was the best thing that ever happened to me. I didn't think I would come back at all."

"Why did you? You had a good thing going in LA. You could have stayed there."

She shrugs and looks around the coffee shop. She looks everywhere but at me. "I guess my biological clock started ticking. I didn't want to spend the rest of my life slaving away at my career. I wanted to find someone and settle down and maybe have a family. That's why I came back."

"Wouldn't it be easier to find someone there? There aren't many people our age left in this town. Everyone leaves."

"Yeah. I know. I don't really know what I'm doing or why I'm here. I sold my company and I decided to come home to figure it out. I figured I needed to see the place where the accident happened and deal with....all the other stuff left over from the accident so I could move on."

"That makes sense," I reply.

"So yeah. The guy in the car was my boyfriend and I haven't really been able to get involved with anyone since. I've dated a few people, but they always seem to disappear before it goes anywhere."

"I'm sorry to hear that."

"Why did you break up with your girlfriend.... or why did she break up with you?"

"She broke up with me," I reply. "She didn't want to do the whole long-distance thing. She wanted us to move in together and take it to the next level."

She snaps out of it quick and studies me with unusual intensity considering how she was just avoiding eye contact with me a second ago. "Why didn't you? You could have moved to Portland to be with her."

"I guess that's kind of the point, isn't it?"

"What is? I don't understand you."

Now it's my turn to shrug and look around at anything but her. This conversation is turning into something I never imagined.

"I guess it got to a tipping point where I could either move away from Oak Falls and live happily ever after with her.... or not. I had to make a choice between her and staying in Oak Falls and I chose to stay."

Jordan gapes at me with her eyes bugging out. "Are you saying that staying in Oak Falls is more important to you than she was? Didn't you care about her at all?"

"I did care about her. I loved her and staying in Oak Falls isn't that important to me—at least, I didn't think it was. I never really made the decision to stay in Oak Falls—not before. I just stayed here because.... well, just because. I stayed because I was already here and had nowhere else I felt compelled to go. Then she threw down this ultimatum that we either had to level up or quit.....and I decided to stay in Oak Falls. It wasn't because Oak Falls was so important to me or because I didn't want to level up with her. It just wasn't compelling enough to make me change my life. I like my life the way it is and I didn't want to change it."

She gazes into my eyes listening to every word. She really drills me with her intensity and I get another thrill. I love the way she focuses her attention on me. She's nowhere else but right here talking to me. I haven't had this in.... well, forever.

I finish talking and she doesn't pick up the conversation. I wind up gazing back at her feeling this flood of emotion I can't define. She's the first girl I've been interested in in a long time. I don't want to walk away and she isn't showing any signs of heading for the hills. Maybe I'm not so much of an asshole.

Just then, Frankie comes over to our table and startles me and Jordan out of our trance. "Can I get you anything?" he asks her.

She jumps and spins around. "Oh! Sorry. Hi, Frankie."

He frowns and then recognizes her. "Jordan? Jordan Cruz? Wow! I haven't seen you in forever."

She stands up and hugs him. He's so genuinely excited to see her that I have to smile at both of them. This is so different from my experience with Anita.

He starts bombarding her with questions. "So what brings you back to town? Are you staying at your parents' place? Are you staying for a while?"

She answers as fast as possible to keep up with him. "Yeah, I guess I'll be here for a while."

Frankie looks down at me and then back at Jordan. "I didn't mean to interrupt. Do you want a drink, Jordan? Your coffee is getting cold, pal."

"I'm okay, Frankie," I tell him. "I've had enough."

"One can never have enough coffee, pal. I keep telling you that."

"I don't need anything, either, Frankie," Jordan tells him. "We were just catching up on everything high school."

"Good times!" He hugs her and walks off. "Call me if you need anything."

He grins at me and disappears into the back. Jordan sits back down. "That guy is the salt of the Earth."

"You better believe it," I reply.

"So where were we when we were so rudely interrupted?" she asks.

"We were both bemoaning the sad state of our love lives."

"Yeah." She giggles. "My love life isn't looking too stellar at the moment."

"How did your date go with Holden?"

She makes a face. "Let's just say you were right about him—not that I didn't suspect. He's....well, let's be diplomatic and say that he isn't interesting or insightful or intriguing or understanding or compassionate or creative or helpful."

"I could have told you that."

"You did tell me that, but the good news is that I found out for myself on our date. So now Holden Keller is in the scrap yard of guys that I don't have a future with."

"Is the scrap yard a big one?"

"Not too big. Most guys don't even make it that far."

I cock my head to study her. "Why is that? Why do you think it never works out?"

She immediately looks away. "I don't know. Maybe I'm damaged goods."

"I'm going to go out on a limb and say that things didn't work out with Holden for some other reason than that. I highly doubt you scrapped him because you're damaged goods."

Her eyes swivel back to me and some of her old spirit flashes in their dark depths. "Do you really think so?"

"You aren't damaged goods. You're intelligent and interesting and insightful and understanding and intriguing and creative and helpful and compassionate. You've shown me all those things just in the time you've been sitting here. How could you possibly be compatible with someone who isn't those things?"

She glances down at the tabletop. "Thanks. I really need to hear that right now."

"Why do you think you're damaged goods—because you got in a car accident? The accident didn't stop you from building a successful company. You seem like you're just fine to me."

"You wouldn't say that if you really knew what I'm like underneath the surface."

"Tell me. Show me." I take a chance and move my hand across the table to hers. I cover her fingers and squeeze. "I want to know."

"No, you don't," she mumbles under her breath. "Trust me. You don't."

"You know all about me," I reply. "Do you think I'm damaged goods?"

Her eyes lock onto mine and a jet of adrenaline scorches into my stomach. "Maybe. I don't know."

"Would you like to go out with me some time and find out?" I ask. "I mean, since you won't be going out with Holden?"

She shrugs. "I don't think I'm in any condition to be going out with anyone."

"You said you came back here to settle down. You said your biological clock was ticking and you wanted to find someone. How are you going to do that if you don't go out with anyone?"

"So you think I'm going to settle down with you?" Her tone gets harsher and her eyes flash dangerously. "Dream on, pal."

"I never said anything about you settling down with me. I just asked if you want to go out sometime. Consider it practice for when you meet the guy of your dreams."

She snorts and picks up her handbag. "I better go. It was nice talking to you."

She leaps out of her chair. I barely stand up in time to keep up with her on her way outside. "Jordan—wait! Don't walk away. I didn't mean to offend you by asking you out. I just.... I really enjoy talking to you. I'd like to talk to you again. That's all I'm saying."

"Talking isn't the same as going out," she clips over her shoulder.

"You went out with Holden because you had nothing else to do. Why couldn't you go out with me for the same reason? It doesn't have to mean anything. What do you say?"

She stops dead on the sidewalk and spins around to glare at me. "Why are you doing this? Why are you trying so hard?"

"I just told you. I like talking to you. You're one of the few people in this town that's taken the time to get to know me. It doesn't have to mean anything. If you don't want to go out sometime, we could just meet up at the overlook or something and keep talking."

"Not there," she snarls under her breath. "Anywhere but there."

"Okay. What about at Ranfurly Park?"

She frowns and then looks away. "All right. Fine."

"When would you be available?"

She studies me even more closely and doesn't answer for what seems like an eternity. She finally purses her lips and says, "I like talking to you, too."

I burst into a huge grin. "Great! Then us talking to each other will be a win for both of us."

"When are *you* available?"

"Whenever. How about now?"

She makes a face. "Fine.

I nod toward the sidewalk and we both start walking. This is not the way I envisioned this conversation going, but who cares?

We reach the park and start walking through it. We aren't talking, but something is definitely happening between us.

I should break the silence, but I can't bring myself to do it. We reach the pond and start walking around it.

She startles me out of my thoughts by murmuring under her breath. "You're interesting."

I jump and then start laughing. "Am I intriguing or helpful or creative?"

"I don't know about that, but you're definitely intelligent, understanding, and compassionate."

I can't help but beam at her. "Thanks. That's high praise coming from you."

"Don't push it too far. I can be cutting and dismissive and standoffish, too."

"I know that." Her eyes are giving me serious butterflies. When did we stop walking? Facing her and looking into her eyes make me impossibly excited and jittery. "I really want to kiss you right now."

She looks away. "That's probably not a good idea."

"Do you want me to kiss you?"

"Why—so you can wind up in the scrap yard with Holden?" She snorts. "You're a glutton for punishment."

"One kiss would be worth winding up in the scrap yard."

She jerks around to glare at me and then her eyes dart down to my mouth. She wants to.

I take a step closer to her. "Please...."

I don't give her a second to hesitate. I kiss her.... lightly. Nothing happens. She doesn't run away, but just for a second there, her lips extended to meet mine and she kissed me back.

I can't stop smiling at her. "What's the verdict? Do you want to scrap me?"

She doesn't soften or smile. What does it actually take to get her to smile?

Without warning, she lunges in and kisses me. She kisses me once and pulls away....and then she's on top of me. She kisses me deep and hot and getting hotter by the second.

I take a split second to realize what's happening and then we're making out big time. I grab her and pull her in hard, but that's nothing compared to what she's doing to me. Her mouth opens and her blistering hot tongue connects with mine.

My head blasts apart as her body touches mine and she slips her hands under my jacket. She rakes her fingertips across my stomach and up my chest and behind my back.

Her body quivers with pent-up energy and her ravenous mouth demands that I kiss her back. Her tongue tastes mind-bendingly sweet and her body collapses against me in luscious, tremulous waves.

I stagger trying to keep up with her hands. I massage the back of her neck steering her mouth into mine and dissolving in those massive, earth-shattering kisses. Fuck, she's so damn hot that I can't stand it.

I feel myself starting to get hard, but when she presses her body into me, she doesn't shy away. She rocks her hips against my pelvis and rides her sweet crotch right against me. She sighs and moans driving herself to the stratosphere.

I can't stand that. I grab her hips and crush her against me. I thrust into her and she shudders with ecstasy. I want her so fucking bad. I want to nail her right here in the park and she's sure acting like she wants that, too.

I slide my hands farther behind her and squeeze two big handfuls of ass. I let my fingers creep deeper between her thighs and pry her legs open. She whimpers for it and crushes her breasts into my chest. I want to tear her apart.

I rip off her mouth and dive into her neck biting fast. I leave hot, wet bites up to her ear and then nuzzle into her shirt collar. I want to rip her clothes off and maul her right now, but her comments at the coffee shop come back to me. Am I being too forward with her? I don't want her to think this is another hit-and-run.

I hesitate and try to ease off, but she only comes at me even faster. She pushes against me and I stumble into a tree. She pins me under her weight, attacks my mouth, and I feel myself losing control.

Her hands burrow under my t-shirt and I groan when she touches my bare skin. I shudder all over as she drags her wicked little fingers over my chest, stomach, and up my sides.

She pulls off just enough for me to see her sex-drunk eyes. "What's wrong?" she husks in a broken whisper.

"Fuck!" I gasp when her fingertips graze me again. My eyes roll back. "Touch me, baby! Don't stop!"

I cover her hand and groan in agony when I press her hot palm into my skin. I can't survive this feeling of her touching me. "Holy fuck, that feels so fucking good!"

She kisses me much more sensually and her eyes drill into my soul watching my reaction to her touch. My package throbs between her legs.

"Do you like that?" she whispers.

"Baby!" I gasp. "I need you so fucking bad! I need you in my mouth right now."

She kisses me again. Her lips and tongue move slower in a dance of blissful rapture. I can almost taste her sweet juices on my tongue.

I force my eyes open to lock on hers. She intoxicates me out of my mind and I have to touch her back. I raise my hand and my fingers close around her breast under her jacket. I squeeze her through her shirt and she moans into my mouth. Her eyes slip out of focus and I ache to take her, but I don't want to trespass on anything.

She rocks her hips harder and faster when I play with her breast through her shirt. She feels magically soft and responsive and her moans match my movements exactly.

She rides harder on my package working herself into a frenzy. I need her so fucking bad!

I slip my hand between her legs and crush her sweet box. "You want me in here, baby?" I whisper. "Is this what you want?"

She groans and drives herself down on my fingers when a gasp makes both of us jolt apart. Jordan freezes in my arms and we both stare at Anita standing thirty feet away. She gapes at us with that same horrified, grisly expression she usually saves just for me. I can read exactly what she thinks about Jordan making out with me in a public park.

Jordan doesn't move for a second. She stays glued to me with her hands still resting against my bare skin. She doesn't make any move to hide the fact that she's rubbing her box against my hand and making me as hard as a rock.

Very, very slowly, she pulls away. Her hands slither out from under my shirt and she turns to face her friend. I don't want to stick around for the aftermath so I walk off into the park without looking back.

Chapter 8: Jordan

I saunter over to Anita waiting for nuclear Armageddon to strike. It's only a matter of time. Walking over there makes me painfully aware of my saturated panties. My whole body zings with energy and desire from making out with Rafe, but I don't regret it. He's hot as hell and I would do it again. I would do a lot more than just make out with him.

I still don't understand why I kissed him like that or why I let it go as far as it did. I would probably have done it with him if Anita didn't show up and interrupt us. I would have let Rafe fuck me in a public park. What am I coming to?

Anita curls her lip at me as I get nearer. Now I know what Rafe has been going through for the past six years. No wonder he doesn't talk to her or order anything from her. No one in their right mind would want to tip a waitress who acted like that.

I'm seeing Anita in a whole new light. Am I just friends with her because she's nice to me? Is it possible that she's this horrible to other people and I just let myself ignore it because her behavior wasn't directed toward me?

She snaps out of it as soon as I get near her. "What on Earth are you doing, Jordan?"

"You can see what I was doing." I walk past her heading back to town. "Don't ask questions you don't want to hear the answers to."

She hustles alongside me talking fast. "How could you do that with him? Do you have any idea who that is?"

"I know who he is, Anita. I know who he is as well as you do."

"He's bad news. He's the worst kind of player. He could have taken advantage of you just now."

"He didn't take advantage of me. If anything, I was the one who took advantage of him....though he didn't try too hard to fight me off."

"You better be careful around him. He's dangerous."

"I think I know a little more about him than you do. You shouldn't jump to conclusions about someone without all the facts."

"What are you talking about? How could you even think about him when you have someone like Holden Keller who wants to go out with you?"

I roll my eyes to Heaven, but I don't stop walking. "I am not going out with Holden Keller ever again."

"Why not? He's a great guy. He's successful and rich and ambitious and popular. He's perfect."

"That's the problem," I mutter over my shoulder.

"What is that supposed to mean? How can you turn your back on him when he's so over the moon about you?"

"Holden doesn't want me. Trust me."

She gasps in horror. "How can you even say that? He's in love with you."

"No, he isn't. He isn't even interested in me."

"Of course he is. What could possibly make you think he isn't interested?"

I whirl around to confront her and pull up my shirt to expose my stomach. "This."

She recoils like she's been slapped. She grimaces in horror at the sight of my scars and immediately turns away. "That isn't funny, Jordan!"

"No, it isn't funny." I set off walking. "Holden isn't interested in me. He isn't interested in finding out who I am or what I'm all about, and if he did find out, he would run in the other direction. I'm the absolute last person in the world that Holden wants and he's the last person in the world that I want. It isn't happening. Sorry."

"Do you have to go for *him* instead?" she moans. "Why does it have to be him of all people? Can't you find someone better?"

"There's nothing going on between me and Rafe," I tell her over my shoulder. "We were just fooling around, and even if there was something going on between us, it would be none of your business. You thought Holden was a good idea and he wasn't. You think Rafe is bad news and we all know how good you are at judging people's characters. You're probably wrong about him, too."

She doesn't answer right away. She strides along at my side as we move through town. I head back to the coffee shop parking lot where I left my car.

"What were you thinking getting all handsy with him in the park?" she growls. "You're really starting to worry me, Jordan."

"Maybe I thought I might as well get laid once in a while since no one is ever going to look sideways at my body ever again. I might as well enjoy myself when I have the chance, and anyways......"

I trail off. I can think of a lot of reasons why I wanted to do it with Rafe. He might not project the outward trappings of success the way Holden does. Rafe is definitely a little rough around the edges.

The fact that he doesn't care about any of that even while being one of the most successful businessmen I've ever met makes him....intriguing.

He's intriguing and intelligent and interesting and insightful and understanding. He's helpful and compassionate. I don't know about being creative and it doesn't look like he's doing great things in the world, but then again, neither am I.

Maybe he doesn't need to be doing great things in the world. He's successful and he's happy with his life the way it is. What could be wrong with that? He's doing a hell of a lot more than most other people.

Anita isn't any of those things. I can't think of one adjective on that list that fits Anita. She's still my best friend.

My parents aren't any of those things, either. My dad is a Police officer, so I guess he's doing some good in the world, but it isn't like he's up to anything big and world-changing. He just does his job, which is something.

I have no reason to judge Rafe's choices. I have no reason to judge his choice in clothes or the way he wears his hair or how he spends his time. He's earned the right to sit on a rock and look at the view while he works on his phone. Who am I to judge that?

He was so obviously distressed when I told him about his past behavior. He's obviously not like that anymore and he carried on a successful relationship for five years. That's a damn sight more than I've ever done. Maybe I could learn something from him.

He isn't my textbook definition of attractive, either, but the way he acts and talks and treats me overshadows that. He's unfailingly kind and attentive. He's been nothing but considerate to me from day one and he's been a thousand times more understanding and compassionate about my situation than Anita ever has been. He's even more understanding and compassionate than my own mother.

Rafe doesn't know about my scars, but something in the way he acts makes me want to believe he would still want me even if he knew.

If he decided to care about me, he wouldn't let my scars stand in the way of whatever developed between us. He couldn't be more different from Holden in that respect.

I don't know how I'd do it with Rafe without him finding out. I don't want him to find out. I don't want anyone to see my scars ever again. I would rather live alone for the rest of my life than face that.

Maybe that's why I initiated it with him and not someone else. Maybe I just wanted to get a quick fix and then never see the person again.

Anita keeps pace with me all the way to the parking lot. She doesn't say anything until we approach my car and I take out my keys. "You aren't going to see him again, are you?"

"I don't know. I might."

She groans and rolls her eyes. "Oh, come on, girlfriend! You could have any guy you want. Why him?"

"You wouldn't understand."

"Why can't you explain it to me, then?"

I study my best friend. I could enlighten her with a few words about how and why Rafe changed. I could explain why he isn't the same person that he was in high school. I could also tell her all about how rich and successful he is and what he does at the coffee shop while he sits there on his phone.

I could change her opinion of him in a matter of seconds. I could make her feel like shit for judging him. I could make her see how rude and heartless she's been to him and I could change the way she treats him when he goes into her place of work each day.

I don't say any of that, though. I keep silent. I want to help Rafe. I want to make his life easier by changing Anita's opinion of him, but I don't feel so inclined to help her out.

She's been cold, cruel, judgmental, and disdainful to him for six years. She had no reason to do any of that apart from her own bias. She's the one who got herself into this and she's the one who will have to get herself out of it. I have no desire to reward her by getting Rafe to tip her for bringing him his coffee every morning.

There really is no excuse at all for her to look down her nose at him, curl her lip at him, and give him the cold shoulder when he comes into the coffee shop. There's no excuse at all for her never to ask him if he wants to order anything. That is just plain inexcusable. Rafe is right about that.

It would be her job to take his order even if he was as bad as we all suspected he was in high school. She would still have to at least take his order even if he was the worst kind of criminal.

She's the one who robbed herself of six years of tips she could have earned from him. I have no desire to save her from that and it isn't my job to make her a good person.

I can't believe I'm even thinking this about my best friend, but Rafe has opened my eyes to a lot of things. I would probably have thought the same things about him if I hadn't taken the time to talk to him. That's what makes me different from her. I talked to him.

I turn away to put my keys in the door lock. "Are you just going to walk away without telling me anything?" Anita asks. "Aren't you even going to talk to me?"

"What would you like me to say? We obviously don't see eye to eye on the subject of guys, so do us both a favor and don't get involved in my love life anymore. Don't set me up with anyone and don't comment on who I go out with or who I do anything with."

Her face pinches and her lip starts to tremble. "But…. we've always talked about that. We've always shared everything with each other."

"Well, I can't share this with you. I'm sorry. Maybe the accident changed me too much, but my love life isn't something I can share with you anymore. I wish it was, but the accident wasn't my fault and whatever changes it brought to my life aren't my fault, either."

Tears brim in her eyes. "Are we still friends?"

"Of course we're friends." Seeing her in distress twists my heart and I put my arms around her. I hug her before I step back. "I gotta go. I'll see you around."

"Can I call you?" Her voice breaks.

"Sure." I pull the door open. "Why don't you come over to my house later since you don't have to work today?"

She whimpers something, but I don't turn around. I need to go off alone and think by myself. No wonder Rafe likes the overlook so much. If it didn't remind me of the accident, it would be the perfect place to go right now.

I move over to the driver's door when a man calls across the parking lot. "Jordan! Wait up!"

I raise my head and cringe when I see Holden striding toward me. He flashes his winning grin and his hair is absolutely motorcycle-helmet perfect. He wears the same suit he had on when he met us at the coffee shop. Maybe it's his only suit. Maybe he's pretending with that, too.

He strolls right up to me, hugs me without asking, and kisses me on the cheek. "It's wonderful to see you again! How are you? Have you given any more thought to our conversation on Friday night? How about we go out again this Friday? We could make Ravenwood Estates our regular Friday night date spot...."

"We aren't going out on Friday night, Holden," I cut in. "We aren't going out this Friday night or next Friday night or any other night. I won't be going out with you again. I'm sorry, but it isn't going to work out."

"Jordan!" Anita hisses.

Holden frowns. This is by far the most authentic reaction I've ever gotten from him. "Would you mind telling me why? I thought we understood each other pretty well on Friday night."

"I understood you very well," I reply. "I understood exactly what you were suggesting and I'm not interested. I'm not the person you're looking for. I'm sorry, but I really think you need to find someone else."

"I don't want someone else. I want you."

"Sorry. It isn't going to happen. It's over." As if it ever started.

Anita lays her hand on my arm. "Maybe we should all just take a moment to think about this...."

"I already thought about it and I've made up my mind. I'm sorry, Holden. I'm not interested in going out with you ever again."

He scowls even more deeply and I turn away. "I gotta go. See you later, girlfriend."

I kiss Anita again and dive into my car. I fire up the engine and pull out of the parking lot so fast that Holden has to leap out of the way to avoid getting run over. Anita can explain to him how badly she messed up with her latest matchmaking catastrophe.

Chapter 9: Jordan

I pull my car up in front of my parents' house, rest my forehead on my hands, and heave a shaky sigh. I came home to Oak Falls because I thought my life couldn't possibly get more screwed up than it already was.

Now it is. It most definitely is more screwed up than it already was. My relationship with my best friend is on the rocks. I just messed around with Rafe Mendoza, one of the most notorious losers in high school, and I just turned down what might be one of the most successful political opportunities of the century.

Who the hell cares about any of that when my life is in the toilet? I really need to pull it together. I just don't know how.

I came back to Oak Falls to change my life. I wanted to shift from high-powered business career woman to trying to find a partner and settle down.

I can't do any of that with these scars. I can't even begin to look for someone until I figure out what I'm going to do about my own body. I could be like this for the rest of my life. I could be worse than this for the rest of my life. Can I really live like that?

I sit up straight and look through the windshield at the dense pine forests surrounding my parents' house. If I can't find a way to accept these scars and move on with my life, what's the point of having a life at all? What's the point of living if I'm too messed up to ever have a relationship.... or children.... or anything? I don't want to live like that.

I shake those thoughts out of my head. I can't start thinking that way. That train of thought only ends one place and I'm not ready to go there yet.

I get out of the car, but when I walk up the steps, I feel how wet my panties are. I haven't reacted to any guy the way I reacted to Rafe.

The sound of him groaning and whining when I touched him....the sight of his eyes rolling back in his head.....that throbbing sensation between his legs.....

All of those things turn me on and flood me with excitement just thinking about them. I would love to do it with him.....but I can't. I don't dare.

I shiver when I remember his raspy whispers of desire. *I need you so fucking bad! I need you in my mouth right now.*

He didn't say anything about pounding me into next week. He didn't say anything about forcing himself on me. He said something about giving me pleasure. He needs to give me that. He asked nothing for himself except to have me touch him.

His body felt amazing under his clothes. He might not be as big or as imposing or as stunning as Holden, but Rafe never acts fake around me—not ever. Every gasp and moan and groan was pure and true and real. He never tried to hide how much he wanted it.

I climb the steps and go inside. My dad sits in his usual armchair reading the paper by the living room window.

"Hi, Dad!" I call through the door.

"Hi, sweetie," he calls back. "How was your trip to town?"

I don't know what to say. What can I say—that I almost fucked Rafe Mendoza in the park?

I couldn't tell my dad that, but when I get ready to go upstairs, I glance through the living room door at him.

He bends over his paper without looking up. He'll never pry or demand answers about why I like Rafe better than Holden. My dad never asks that, but the sight of him brings up a whole lot of questions I can't answer.

I put down my handbag and stroll into the living room. I stand ten feet off and watch my dad reading the paper. He's a Police officer. He knows more than anyone about what goes on in this town.

"Dad...." I begin.

He doesn't look up. "Mmm-hmmmm?"

"I need to ask you something."

"Go ahead."

"Could you find out about someone for me? Could you do some digging on someone and tell me about them?"

He freezes ever-so-slightly, but a second later, he relaxes and goes back to what he's doing. "You know I can't do that, sweetie."

"But you know everyone in Oak Falls. You know more than anyone I can think of about everyone in town. How else am I supposed to find out if someone is dangerous or if they're telling the truth about who they are?"

He flips the page and pretends to keep reading. "Who do you want to find out about?"

I gulp. "Rafe Mendoza."

He finally looks up at me. "What do you want to know about him?"

"He says he suffered a head injury and lost his memory. He says he was found wandering around with no memory of who he was before or how he got like that. EMS took him to the hospital which means the Police Department should have a record of the call."

"You know all of that information is totally confidential, darling. I couldn't tell you even if I knew."

"Are you saying you know whether it's true?"

"I can't tell you that, sweetie. It's all sealed under medical confidentiality."

"Do you know if Rafe ever got in trouble with the law? Do you know if he ever got busted for drugs.... or for being violent.... with women?"

My dad's intense scrutiny makes me cringe. I'm really going way too far with this line of questions and why should I bother when I already believe Rafe? Do I really want my dad to tell me that Rafe lied about everything?

Anita was right about one thing. Rafe could have done anything to me in that park. If he was going to prove that he's the same violent asshole he was in high school, he would have done it then.

My dad raises his paper in front of his face. "Whatever Rafe Mendoza did or didn't do in the past and whatever might or might not be on Rafe Mendoza's criminal record is none of your business, darling. You should know better than to go sticking your nose into other people's business."

"It's my business if there's a chance I could get involved with him. If you know something about him that could put me in danger, don't you have a responsibility to me as your daughter to warn me in advance? Do you know anything about Rafe that could make me question whether it's a good idea to have anything to do with him? Please tell me, Dad."

He lowers his paper and skewers me over the top edge. His eyes go hard—much harder than I can ever remember before.

I shuffle my feet and brace myself for another reprimand. I shouldn't be asking my dad about any of this—certainly not about guys I might or might not be getting intimately involved with.

My dad is the only person I can think of that I trust enough to tell me the truth. My dad will be the one who knows whatever Rafe might or might not have been doing in Oak Falls since high school. My did is also the only person with a legitimate reason to tell me the truth.

He lowers his paper very slowly and trains his hard eyes on me. "I will tell you one thing about Rafe Mendoza, darling, and please do me a favor and make this the last time you ever ask me about him or any other guy you might be interested in."

"Okay, Dad," I quaver. "I won't ask again."

"I can only tell you one thing about him and it's this. He's the only man in Oak Falls that I would feel totally comfortable with you going out with."

I stare at him trying to grasp what the hell he just said. My dad is the best judge of character I've ever met. He can size up a person in seconds and he always judges correctly.

He's the polar opposite of Anita, but my dad never flaunts this hidden talent of his. He never tells anyone what he really thinks of anyone. He just sees and knows and understands a person's worth from the moment he first lays eyes on them.

I get a flashback to that afternoon at the overlook. My dad saw Rafe sitting on the rock and my dad never once tried to stop me from going out there. He must have seen me and Rafe talking to each other.

No decent father would let his daughter talk to someone who was dangerous or had a bad reputation. My dad would have stopped it or called me back to the car much sooner if he didn't want me talking to Rafe.

Now my dad is telling me that Rafe is the only man in town that he wouldn't mind seeing me go out with. I get another flashback to the night Holden picked me up for our date. My dad didn't try to stop me from going out with Holden, but my dad didn't exactly welcome Holden with open arms.

One thing I know for certain. My dad would never have let me go out with Holden if my dad didn't know implicitly that I would see Holden for what he was. My dad had no reason to stop me from going out with Holden. My dad already knew that I would find out for myself what Holden was really about.

My dad is too smart to steer me toward the man he wants me to get with. My dad never would have said a damn word about Rafe if I didn't pry it out of him.

My dad makes sure I get the message loud and clear before he raises his paper and goes back to reading it. He pretends I'm not there, but I can't stop staring at him. He knows something—something important—something way more important than how Rafe lost his memory.

It would have to be something massive for my dad to come to this opinion about Rafe. Does my dad know about Rafe's wealth....or his relationship.....or is it something else?

My dad won't tell me anything else and I gave him my promise not to ask. I'll just have to find out about Rafe on my own.

Chapter 10: Rafe

I hoist a heavy timber onto my shoulder, climb up the ladder to the roof, and drop the beam on the exposed framing. I balance on the few solid cross joists, pull my hammer from my tool belt, and start fitting the beam into place.

I have to strain to position it and then I have to bring up my circular saw to cut the joint angles. I stretch my back for a second and catch my breath while I fish the nails out of my pouch.

I put five nails in my mouth and start hammering when I hear a car coming up the road. I don't pay any attention at first. Cars are always passing on the road farther down the mountain. They don't come up here.

I pound a few more nails, and when I stop to take out some more, I hear the car coming closer. There's no doubt about it. The car is definitely coming toward my house.

Mine is the only house at the end of the road. No one comes up here unless they're seriously lost and that hasn't happened in ages.

I move over to a different section of the roof and drive three more nails before the car shows up. I don't want to climb all the way down to the ground just to give someone directions back to Oak Falls. I can do that from here and I'm busy.

The car appears around the last curve and I squint down as it pulls in front of the house. I stay squatting on the timbers and rest my elbow on my knee waiting for the driver to get out.

I freeze and my heart flips when Jordan gets out of the car wearing a loose, flowing summer dress. She shades her eyes and peers up at me. "What are you doing up there?"

"Fixing the roof. What are you doing down there?"

She blushes and tries not to smile, but it sneaks out anyway. One of these days, I'm going to make her smile for real and then look out.

"I'm looking for you," she tells me, "but it looks like I found you."

"Here I am. What can I do for you? Are you sure I'm not too dangerous for you to talk to?"

She laughs, but she still tries to hold it back. "Anita told me a whole bunch of horror stories about this place." She makes a face at the house. "This place is a dump. How can you live here?"

"I don't live here. I live up there." I point my hammer up the mountain. She follows the gesture and sees my cabin tucked into the trees. It's barely visible in the shadows.

She stands there with her back to me taking in the scene and then turns around to frown at the house. She can see from where she stands that most of the roof is caving in. Half the walls are so rotten that she can see straight through them to the decrepit rooms inside. Someone would take their lives in their hands to set foot on the floor.

"Anita says you lived here with your dad before he died."

"I did." I bend down and drive two more nails.

"You lived here—in this?" She makes a face. "Wow. That sounds terrible."

"It wasn't as bad as this when I was growing up. My dad got sick after I came home from the hospital. He lived in the back room over there." I point to the corner of the house behind me. "He almost never left it and he used to get really annoyed if I tried to fix anything."

"So what did you do?"

"I built that cabin so I'd have a decent place to live. I used to come down here to take care of him, and when he died, I started fixing the place up. It used to be a lot worse."

"Worse!" she shrieks. "How could it be worse?"

"I tore out all the old rotten walls and started working on the roof. I haven't gotten around to the floor yet. It takes a long time when I'm doing everything myself."

"Why don't you hire some construction guys to do it for you? You could have it all done in a few weeks."

"I like doing it myself. It relaxes me and gives me something to work on that doesn't involve a screen. Besides, I like spending time up here by myself and I already have a decent place to live. I'm in no hurry and I don't really have a use for a house this big."

She stands off and surveys the house. It really is a disaster zone. I'll be the first to admit that, but at least it's mine.

She watches me pound my nails and I finally get the beam fitted into place. It's time for the next one, but when I climb down the ladder, she comes over to me. "How have you been?"

"I'm good. How are you? Did Anita have a tantrum when she saw you kissing me?"

She tries to suppress laughter. "I wouldn't call it a tantrum."

"What would you call it?"

"Full di-lithium warp core meltdown."

I have to laugh and I don't want to walk away from her to go back up on the roof. I'm already down here talking to her so I might as well stay here.

She smiles at me when I laugh and then her eyes skip down my body to my clothes. My shirt is saturated with sweat and my jeans are torn and covered in sawdust.

I can't read her reaction, but that look makes me uncomfortable. She doesn't turn up her nose at me, but she's seeing me in a way that no one in town has ever seen me before. I would never go into town looking like this and I definitely would never let a girl I'm interested in see me like this.

I unbuckle my tool belt and lay it on the pile of timbers. I walk away from her pulling off my shirt and I toss that into the bed of my pickup truck. I walk over to the hose faucet, turn on the hose, and spray the water over my head to soak myself down. I should really take a shower, but I don't want to leave her alone for that long.

I turn around to find her staring at me with that piercing intensity of hers. I realize out of the clear blue sky that I have my shirt off in front of her and water all over myself.

I duck into the back of the house and come back out drying myself with a towel. I stop in front of her and pull on a clean shirt. "So what did you want to find me for?"

"I wanted to talk to you about your head injury."

"I already told you everything. Do you need me to go downtown for the full Police interrogation?"

"I already asked my dad about you and he said it was none of my business, so I figured I'd come and get the details straight from the horse's mouth."

"I already told you everything I know. I don't remember anything else and what I do know I learned from my dad."

"So what do you remember?"

"My earliest memories are from a brain injury clinic in Seattle. My dad told me that I was in a coma for about six weeks after they found me, but my ability to remember anything or understand what was happening didn't come back until months later. I guess my brain got scrambled and I couldn't process anything even though I was awake."

"Did your dad say where you were found?"

"No."

"Did he say *when* you were found?"

"Nope. It was months after the injury happened. None of that seemed important by then. I don't know if he asked the Police or if they ever told him, but he didn't mention it and I don't think I ever asked. I had enough to worry about just relearning how to tie my shoes and go to the bathroom."

"But you remembered how to trade. You said you started in high school."

"I started trading in the hospital. I had nothing else to do so I learned that."

She looks away. "Damn. That doesn't leave much to go on, does it?"

"What do you want to know all that for?"

She shrugs. "I don't know."

"Do you believe me that I had a head injury?"

She turns around and her eyes lock on me. "I have only your word that you had a head injury. No one else was around and my dad won't tell me anything about whether the Police have a record of the call. I've searched the internet and I can't find out anything about it."

"Dr. Patterson knows about it. You could ask him."

"The injury would be covered by medical confidentiality. He won't tell me anything, either."

"I can give him permission to tell you. I can take you to see him and I can instruct him to give you all the information you want. I can even let you see my medical file if that helps."

She studies me a little more closely if that's even possible.

"Why is it so important to you to know whether I'm telling the truth? You didn't seem too concerned with it yesterday when we were making out in the park."

"No. I wasn't."

"So what changed?"

"I don't know. Maybe I just need to obsess about something other than my own sorry existence for a change."

"Why is your existence sorry? You have everything going for you. You have incredible talent. You have business know-how. You're beautiful and smart and..."

"Intelligent and intriguing and interesting and understanding and helpful and compassionate?" She smirks. "You're really nice."

"Was I really nice in high school? How do you think I got like this if I didn't have a head injury?"

"I don't doubt that you had a head injury. I don't really know why I'm asking."

I wave up to the cabin. "Do you want to come up and have some lunch with me? I was just about to knock off."

She glances at her watch. "It's three o'clock in the afternoon."

"Okay. Forget lunch. Come have a drink with me."

"Okay." She starts following me up the hill toward the cabin. "So what happened to your dad?"

"Diabetes. He didn't take care of himself and let himself crumble into an early grave."

"I'm sorry to hear that."

"Don't be."

"Do you miss him? Don't you get lonely out here without someone?"

I glance down at her to find her eyes glowing up at me. "The only thing I miss is maybe some of the physical intimacy of having a girlfriend. I don't miss anything else."

"What about companionship? Don't you miss sharing your life with someone like that? Do you always have to be alone?"

"No one has ever asked me these questions before."

"That's sad. Maybe you don't miss it because you've never had it."

"You're right. I've never had it, not even with my old girlfriend. Maybe that's why I found it so easy to let her end the relationship. I didn't feel like I was losing anything except the regular kissing and sex. I didn't think that was worth losing all of this."

"This?" She pauses to scan the property. "There's nothing here."

"I mean the feeling of being my own master. No one tells me what to do here. I have everything I need—except for the regular kissing and sex. I'm happy here. I have all the money I need. I don't need anything else, but if I did, I can get it. I'm the master of my destiny and I decide what I do and when. I wasn't willing to trade that for kissing and sex."

"Wow," she breathes. "That sounds incredibly sad."

"Why? What's sad about it?"

"It's sad that you didn't have that close connection with her. Imagine if you felt like she was the missing half of your soul—like you could never be complete without her in your life. Imagine if you felt like you couldn't even know yourself without the bond between you and nothing in life would ever be the same without her."

I find myself studying her with the same intensity. She's telling me something—something beyond important. "Have you ever had that?"

She nods into the distance and won't look at me.

"You said no one has ever lasted. How could you know that such a thing existed if you never experienced it for yourself?"

She gulps. "His name was Raleigh—Raleigh Sinclair. He was the driver of the car that crashed. He was my high school boyfriend and we were planning to get married and move to LA together as soon as we graduated."

I don't know what to say. She looks impossibly sad talking about him even though he died so many years ago.

"This is the first time since the accident that I've ever even thought about trying to find that again," she mumbles under her breath. "I never let myself think it could ever happen like that again, but if I'm going to try to get with someone and start a family, I want it to be like that."

She jumps a foot in the air and whips around when I open the cabin door. I wave her inside and shut it behind us both when we step inside.

She wanders around taking in the scene while I go over to the kitchen. Big windows give a view off the living room to the mountains behind my dad's old house. Sunshine beams through the skylights and shines on the heavy wooden timbers, the loft bedroom over the kitchen, and the wood-burning stove in the corner.

This cabin isn't much bigger than a standard-sized car garage, but it's comfortable and it's mine. It's a damn sight more comfortable than my dad's house was even when he was alive.

I get a bottle of juice out of the fridge, pour two glasses, and take them over to her. She stands at the window and looks out at the view. She jumps again when I tap her elbow to get her attention.

I hand her the glass. "Now I understand why you haven't been able to keep a guy around....and it isn't because you're damaged goods. You just haven't found the right guy."

She shrugs and goes back to looking out the window. "Thanks. I sure wish I could get him back."

"I wish I could get my memory back, but I guess life has other plans for us."

I sip my drink, and after another long pause, she does the same. She turns around and casts another critical eye over my cabin. "I can see now that you really are creative."

"What do you mean?"

"Did you build this place all by yourself?"

"I had to. I couldn't live down there with all the rot and filth."

"You didn't have to make it so beautiful."

I raise my eyebrows. "You think it's beautiful?"

"Of course it is. It's one of the nicest houses I've ever seen."

"I'm glad you think so. It makes it worth it that you like it." She studies me even more closely. "What is it that you see when you look at me like that? You've been looking at me like that since we first met."

"I'm just trying to figure you out."

She stares at me so intently that I can't look away. I search her eyes for some clue what she's thinking. Why does my story fascinate her so much?

I hold her gaze as steadily as I can. I want her to find whatever it is she wants to find in me. I don't want her to look away.

She takes one more sip of her drink. She's barely touched it. Then she sets her glass on the coffee table and walks up to me. "You're right. I didn't come up here to find out about your head injury."

I almost ask her what she means when she takes my glass away from me and comes at me kissing me just as ravenously as she did in the park.

She glides her arms around my neck and pushes me backward. I hit the kitchen counter before I react and meet her kissing her back. Her passion doesn't surprise me as much now that I've kissed her and touched her in the park.

I grab her and tighten my fists in her dress. I crush her against me and I don't hesitate to shove my swelling crotch into her.

She explodes with all her massive energy and practically climbs up my body kissing me with everything she has. She grinds her hips against my waist and drags my shirt up so she can touch my stomach.

That feeling blows me apart and I grab hold of her hips to pull her in. I want her so fucking bad, and from the way she keeps pawing at me, she wants it, too. This must be why she came up here—so we can finish what we started in the park without Anita interrupting.

She rips off my mouth and yanks my shirt over my head. She touches me all over and makes me gasp. Her hands set me on fire and I dive under her dress. I scoop my hands up her thighs and lift her off the floor.

She wraps her legs around me nipping my lips with her teeth and cramming her tongue into my mouth. Fuck, she turns me on so much!

I turn her around to put her on the kitchen counter and change my mind. I stumble over to the wall and pin her there while I rip down her collar along with her bra.

Her beautiful apple breasts fall into my hands and I guide them into my mouth. Her delicious whimpering sobs shatter my brain when she buries her hot lips in my ear. She drives me out of my mind and I can't stop drilling my throbbing crotch between her legs.

She rides down on me clawing at my hair and back and chest. She's a wild animal in desperate need and I want to give her everything she wants.

She arches her back against the wall to welcome me between her legs. She undulates in such exquisite, excruciating waves that I can't stop. I need to get inside her—now.

She drives one arm down between us and I groan in agony when her strong little fingers close around my junk through my jeans. She crushes me in deep, brutal squeezes that nudge me to the brink of insanity.

I drag my eyes open to find her searching my innermost being. What does she see? Does she like making me groan like this?

All at once, she pushes me back, drops her feet to the floor, and turns her face to the wall. She doesn't let go of my package and she pulls me against her. Holy fuck, she wants it like that!

I attack her in all my ferocious need. I've never needed anyone this badly and not because I haven't had anyone in a year. Something about her triggers my deepest instincts to possess her.

I smother her with my weight panting into her ear, biting her neck, and flexing my knees to push into her from behind. She whines and yelps every time I bite her, but she also pushes back against my thrusts to urge me onward.

I grab her hands and plant them on the wall, but a second later, she seizes my hands and guides them around her from behind. She steers one to her breasts and the other between her legs. She buries my fingers inside her and my mind dissolves in the wetness of her endless desire.

Chapter 11: Jordan

I can't think as Rafe takes hold of me from behind. I feel his hardness getting closer to the moment of truth. He rips up my dress and plunges his fingers deep inside me. I can't stand much more of this before I explode.

He rasps in my ear teasing me to insanity. "Fuck, yeah, baby!" he husks. "Fuck, yes! You want me, don't you? Do you want me to take you like this, baby?"

I can only whimper and moan as he fingers me out of my mind. His other hand pinches my nipples and makes me yelp. Every commanding thrust triggers an instinctive reaction so that I push back into his rhythm.

I feel him turning me into a wild animal. I want that. I want him to consume me and take me out of myself. I want to feel that he wants me in the most primitive, visceral way.

His fingers propel me closer to a mind-destroying cataclysm and I hear myself starting to scream. If he doesn't stop, he'll make me orgasm right here on his hand and then what will I do?

He seems to realize what's happening and dives in trying to reach my mouth to kiss me. He bites my neck and then along my cheek, but he can't reach me.

He pulls his hand out from between my legs, grips the back of my neck, and steers my mouth the rest of the way to his. I'm so close now that I can't control what I do. I surrender completely to his control and moan into his devouring lips. No one has ever made me this ravenous before. He does something to me that I can't understand.

He keeps smothering me with kisses that I can't stop. He turns me closer to him, and when I can't turn any further, he lifts his weight off me and rotates me back around to face him.

He attacks me kissing me so fucking hard and fast and hot that I can barely breathe. I can't stop moaning as he picks me up and plunges between my legs. He pulls my dress up, tugs my panties aside, and in a split second, he drives into me.

The first thrust satisfies so much bottomless, heart-aching need that I disintegrate in the greatest climax of my life right there. I collapse in a melting puddle of release, but he's just getting started.

He drives me up the wall with his powerful, deep, catastrophic thrusts. I can't stop screaming except that he muffles the sound with atomic kisses. How is he doing this to me?

His hands crawl up the wall next to my head and he arches his body into me like he might be trying to smash the wall down with his pumps. He never lets me fall, and when he glides out for his next stroke, I sink down on his masterful shaft with another agonized scream of fulfillment.

I hear him roaring into my mouth as he picks up speed and power. His muscles strain and he can barely kiss me anymore. His frenzied eyes look at something beyond me even as he looks into the deepest corner of my being.

All at once, he stabs in and holds there howling into my mouth. His body shudders all over and that crushing intensity of his climax sets me off. I can't stop screaming as wave upon wave of ecstasy floods me coming from him. What is he doing to me? How can I ever be the same after this?

He gives one last tortured groan and shivers all over before he snaps back to reality. He's looking at me now—only at me. His lips come back to life and he starts kissing me much more sensually, slowly, and deliciously.

He eases off enough for me to put my feet on the floor and my dress falls between us. He gives one last satisfied gasp, but he doesn't take his hands off the wall. He stands there framing me with his body and kissing me. Will he ever stop? He doesn't act like he wants to.

His body is much leaner and wirier than I expected. He keeps it covered up with his jacket, but now I see that he's powerfully built, though not as bulky as some gym rats I've seen.

He has a much harder, more rugged, dangerous physique that comes from hard work. He isn't a cellphone warrior—as if I could ever think that about him.

His mouth goes unbelievably soft when he kisses me and his eyes shine with so much understanding and compassion that I can hardly stand it.

He eventually straightens up and takes one hand off the wall, but only to stroke my cheek and run his fingers through my hair. He does everything slowly and deliberately like he wants to cherish every minute. I don't know how to react to this. It isn't what I expected at all.

I don't know what I expected, but a second later, he turns away, takes my hand, and leads me over to the couch. It's a deep, dark-brown leather sofa facing the huge windows. Everything about this cabin has the same solid, comfortable, rustic quality that puts me instantly at ease.

He sits me down, sits down next to me, and hands me my glass of juice. I wasn't interested in it before, but now I find that I'm really thirsty. I croak out, "Thanks," and then drink it.

He rests his elbows on his knees and watches me from close range. "I don't want you to think I did this just to use you. I don't want you to think this was just a way for me to get what I want from you and then throw you out. I don't want you to think that."

I glance at him and try to look away, but I can't when I see his eyes gleaming. Those eyes demand my whole attention.

He puts his arm around my shoulders, hugs me, and kisses the side of my head. "That was incredible—the best I've ever had. I've never done it like that with anyone before."

I look down into my glass. I don't know what to say.

"Did you enjoy that?" he asks. "Did you like it?"

I nod, but I can't just sit here in silence and let him wonder. "Maybe I was the one who used you."

He surprises me out of my mind when he bursts out laughing. He hugs me tighter and jostles me good-naturedly. "You can use me anytime you want, baby. Anytime you need an itch scratched, I want to be the first guy you call."

My head snaps up fast. "You don't really mean that."

"If you want me, I'm all yours. You know where I live."

I look away. "I couldn't do that to you."

"You just did. It was great. I would do it again."

"I mean.....I wouldn't want you to think I was....you know.....that I disrespected you for doing it."

I try to look back down into my juice, but he cups my chin and lifts my head to make me look at him. He takes way too long to lean in and kiss me. "You are incredible. You are beautiful. You are magical and powerful and delicious. I want you—always. I would love it if you drove up here in the middle of the night, crawled into my bed, took advantage of me, and then vanished into the shadows. I would love it if I knew that you wanted me half as much as I want you or that I could give you even half as much pleasure as you give me."

I don't know what to say. I can only stare into his eyes. He really means it. He would let me have my way with him and never ask for anything in return.

I finally force myself to gulp and manage to choke out the words, "I loved it. It was wonderful."

He bursts into a huge smile. "And it doesn't bother you that I don't remember anything from high school?"

"No. It doesn't bother me."

"Do you want to spend the night?"

My jaw drops. Did he just say that?

He laughs again. "Don't look so shocked. You can stay as long as you want to. I'd love to have you....stay, I mean."

I tear myself away. "I should probably get home. My parents are expecting me home for dinner."

"Okay. You're welcome to come back anytime. If I'm not here, just wait and I'll see you when I get here."

The words get stuck in my throat. Is he seriously suggesting that I could treat him as a casual plaything whenever I want? It sure sounds like that's what he's saying. Does he really mean that I could just roll in, do it with him, and leave?

I don't know what to make of this or even if I should make anything of it. I don't know if I could bring myself to come back here, not even for sex as mind-blowing as what we just did.

I find myself looking around his cabin. It's one of the nicest, most comfortable houses I've ever set foot in. Knowing that he built it all himself makes it even more amazing. He really is creative....and he's doing great things in the world. He's just doing them where no one else can see.

I must be the first woman who has ever come to visit him here. He said he always visited his ex-girlfriend in Portland. She never came up here. I'm the first woman he's ever done it with in this cabin.

Does that mean something I should be worried about? How could it when he just said I could show up in the middle of the night, take advantage of him, and then disappear?

He doesn't wait for me to figure it out. He stands up, takes my hand, and leads me to the door. He pauses just long enough for me to put my empty glass on the kitchen counter before he leads me back down the hill to my car.

He kisses me long and slow before I get into the driver's seat. "Thanks for stopping by," he murmurs. "I really like having you around."

"Yeah," I breathe. "I really like hanging out with you."

There doesn't seem to be anything left to say so I get in my car and drive away. I drive back to my parents' house and sit in the driveway for a while trying to think.

I just did it with Rafe Mendoza. We did it against his living room wall and I loved it. Just thinking about it makes my stomach hurt with aching desire to do it again. I get even more turned on when I fantasize about sneaking into his bed and letting our bodies take over. That would be fantastic.

Would I ever have the courage to do something like that? He makes me want to, but this nagging doubt keeps holding me back. What if he saw my scars? What would he think?

I could sneak in under cover of darkness and do it with him with the light off. He would never see, just like he didn't see this time.

Is that what I want—anonymous sex in the dark with someone who doesn't see or know about my flaws?

That isn't what I told him I wanted. That isn't finding the missing half of my soul that I couldn't be complete without. That isn't creating a bond with someone—the bond so strong that nothing in life would ever be the same without him.

I don't even know if he wants that. He's never had it so maybe he doesn't think he needs it. He hasn't gone to any great lengths to get it and he's never told me that he wants it with anyone. He just keeps talking about us having casual sex.

I get out of the car, go inside, and spot my dad in his chair by the living room window. "Hi, Dad!" I call out.

"Hi, sweetheart!" he calls from behind his paper.

I go up to my room and open my laptop. I continue my internet searches on Rafe and find more than I ever wanted to know about the time he spent in various hospitals and rehabs all over the Pacific Northwest.

There are even a couple of articles about events he participated in at school…. before he started wasting his life with other losers in high school.

I still can't find what I'm looking for, though. None of this satisfies my curiosity or answers the questions nagging me about him.

I widen my search and discover that he's a stakeholder in some very big, very lucrative real estate investment trusts. Deeper digging turns up his name on property sales ranging into the multimillion-dollar price range, so he told the truth about that, too.

I sit back staring at the screen. I don't know what else I'm supposed to look at, so I scroll back through news articles from the Oak Falls *Monthly*. I don't know what I'm going to find here that I don't already know.

I can't even define exactly what I'm looking for. So far, everything on the internet confirms Rafe's story about how his head injury changed his life.... for the better.

I lose steam and wind up flipping through *Monthly* issues going all the way back to......

I freeze when I turn another page and wind up looking at the headline about Raleigh Sinclair's death. There it is, all laid out in livid, lurid color.

The paper shows pictures of the car crumpled to a pancake at the bottom of the ravine. Of course the Medical Examiner had already removed Raleigh's body by the time the picture was taken and I was in the hospital getting my body put back together.

I stare at the picture for what seems like eons. Of course my parents, friends, and neighbors would never show me this picture before. Life was hard enough after losing Raleigh and getting nearly torn in half during the accident.

This is so much worse than looking down the mountain from the overlook. This article makes the accident so much more real. I swallow hard trying to hold myself together. I can't fall apart now. The accident was six years ago. Why do I still let it affect me so much?

I turn away feeling disgusted with myself. I shouldn't even be looking at this. I flip to the next page. Nothing. There's no further mention of Raleigh or me. The accident just vanished from everyone's awareness. I'm the only one still tormenting myself about it.

I turn another page and start reading an article about our high school football team, the Oak Falls Lumberjacks, taking the regional championships thanks to the spectacular leadership of team captain Holden Keller.

A big picture at the top shows Holden in all his toothy victorious glory. He was as glowing and attractive then as he is now except that his smile looks much more genuine. He hadn't committed himself to full-blown fakery yet. That was a few years down the road for him.

I'm just about to turn the page when I see it. A tiny snippet all the way at the bottom of the page catches my eye, but not because I'm in it or because it mentions Holden or Rafe.

The name that sticks out and makes my hair stand on end is Isaac Cruz.

Police Officer Isaac Cruz discovered a young Oak Falls High School student wandering alone on Desolation Heights Road in the early hours of Sunday morning. The student, whose identity has been withheld due to his age, suffered a head injury of unknown origin and Officer Cruz transported the student to Oak Falls Hospital where the student was airlifted to Portland Medical Center for treatment. The Police Department is asking anyone with knowledge of this incident to come forward to aid the investigation.

I fight down a surge of panic reading the article over and over again. This notice came out less than forty-eight hours after Raleigh drove off the overlook—the overlook on Desolation Heights Road.

My dad was the one who found Rafe wandering alone on the same road where Raleigh drove his car off the road. My dad found Rafe less than two miles away from the ravine.

I can only think of one way Rafe could have gotten his head injured on that road in the middle of the night. Someone was up there at the time of the accident. Someone called EMS, pulled me from the wreck, saved my life on Desolation Heights Road, and then vanished off the face of the Earth.

It had to be Rafe. He was there at the time of the wreck. He must have gotten hurt pulling me out of the car and back up onto the road. He's the person who saved my life.

I keep blinking at the screen reading the lines again and again. I can't believe it. Am I the only person who realizes?

Rafe doesn't know. He didn't recognize me. He must have gotten hurt after he pulled me from the car. How did it happen? Did he fall down the ravine after he pulled me to safety? Did he get hit by another car? Did he trip and fall before the wreck and then the head injury damaged his brain after he made it back up to the road?

I'll never know the answers to any of those questions, and what's even worse, he'll never be able to tell me. No one will. He's completely in the dark.

One thing I know for sure now. He saved my life before he lost his memory. He didn't call EMS after he lost his memory. He didn't climb down that ravine with a life-threatening head injury that scrambled his brain and made him forget everything.

He was the person who saved my life before he lost his memory. He must have been a good person before the accident. He might have been a troubled, violent player, but he was still good enough to want to save me.

He could have died pulling me from that wreck and he did it anyway. He wasn't a creep and an asshole at all. The person he is now was still there before he lost his memory.

Just then, my mom startles me by calling from downstairs. "Dinner's ready, Jordan! Anita's here to have dinner with us."

"I'm coming, Mom!" I yell back.

I leap out of my seat and race downstairs. God only knows how I'm going to get through this meal without losing my mind.

I pass the living room. I stop on the threshold to study my dad sitting in his chair reading the paper.

He looks up and his eyes meet mine. He knows. Now I know why Rafe is the only man in town that my dad would be happy to see me going out with. Rafe saved my life. My dad was the one who found him wandering around on Desolation Heights Road. My dad must have put two and two together. That's why he didn't mind me talking to Rafe at the overlook.

My dad smiles at me and I smile back. I know and he knows. That's enough. No one else needs to know, not even Rafe himself.

Chapter 12: Rafe

I glance up from my phone when I hear the doorbells jangle at the Daily Grind Coffee Shop. My stomach drops when Jordan walks in. She smiles at me and then at Anita, who stands behind the counter serving another customer.

I lower my eyes expecting Jordan to go talk to Anita, but instead, she veers toward my chair and plunks down in the chair right next to me. She puts her handbag on the floor, beams at me, and then tugs her chair closer so she's sitting right next to me.

I can hardly believe my eyes when she gives me a huge, beaming, glorious, radiant smile. "Hi."

"Um....hi....." I stammer. "Are you sure you're allowed to be seen with me in public?"

She bursts out laughing loud enough for her voice to ring through the coffee shop. Everyone turns around to look, especially Anita.

I can't stop staring at Jordan. I've been itching to make her laugh and smile like that, but I gave up on evet getting her to do it.

Now she won't stop blasting me with so much sunshine that I don't know what to think. Did having sex with me make her this happy? She wasn't acting like this when she left my house. She acted like she might never come near me again.

She rests her elbow on her chair arm, props her chin in her hand, and leans toward me grinning like anything.

"Um.... are you okay?" I glance toward Anita who glares at the two of us as venomously as ever. "Do you need something?"

"I just wanted to see you. Do you want to go out with me sometime?"

My eyes fall out of their sockets. "You mean...."

"Do you want to go on a date—dinner or something? I could pick you up and I'll pay and everything....since I'm the one asking you out. This is the twenty-first century, you know. I'm allowed to do that."

"Um.... ooookkkkkaaaayyy...." I frown at her. "Are you sure? Who are you and what have you done with Jordan Cruz?"

She laughs again. "So is that a yes?"

"Yes. I'll go out with you, but I'd rather drive and pay and everything. I'm old-fashioned that way."

She couldn't look more delighted. "Okay. Are you going to drive me in your truck?"

"Is that okay? I don't have another car."

"It's fine." Her eyes twinkle in a way that tells me she really doesn't give a crap if I drive her on a date in my ratty old truck. She doesn't care about anything except going out with me. Something is going on here.

"Did something happen between yesterday and now?"

"Yeah. What happened is that I want to go out with you. Do you want to decide where we go or do you want me to decide? Just don't take me to the restaurant at Ravenwood Estates. Holden took me there and I really don't want to go back."

"Okay. I won't take you there."

"Great!" She bursts into another grin.

Her cheery demeanor is really starting to unnerve me. "Are you okay?" I ask again.

"I'm great. Do you want me to get out of here so you can get back to trading? I don't mind. Just tell me if you need to work."

"I don't need to." I put my phone away. "How are you? Are you in town for something or did you just come to see me?"

"I just came to see you...to ask you out. I considered sneaking into your room in the middle of the night, but I thought this would be the more chivalrous way to ask you out—less like a creepy user taking advantage of you."

She laughs at her own joke. I can't stop staring at her. "Chivalrous! You were trying to be chivalrous....to me?"

"I know a guy is supposed to be chivalrous to a girl, but I figured I should probably offer the olive branch after everything that happened at the park and then at your place. I thought it would be better if I went about it in a more....shall we say.....respectful way."

"You weren't being disrespectful to me. I told you I enjoyed it."

"I know you said that, but I still feel like I went about it the wrong way. I regret now that I didn't accept when you asked me out before. I pushed you away and that was a mistake." I open my mouth to argue back, but she holds up her hand to stop me. "Please. Just accept my apology and let's forget it. I don't want to dwell on it anymore. I'm sorry. I'd like to go out with you—the right way—not using you or anything like that."

"Okay. I'd like that."

She smiles even more broadly. "So how's the roof coming?"

I shrug. "I was thinking about what you said about getting someone else to do it. I don't really need to do it myself."

"You said you enjoyed doing it yourself."

"I do, but I realized that I've only been satisfied to do it slowly because I've never had a reason to get it done before."

"What reason would make you want to do it quickly?"

"I don't know. Maybe.....sharing it with someone." I give her a significant look.

She blushes furiously. "You're really sweet, but your cabin is so beautiful. It's a place anyone would want to share with you."

"Would you want to share it with me?"

She turns bright red and looks away. "I think we should maybe go out a few times before we start asking that."

"But if we did go out a few times and things did go there between us, is it somewhere you would like to share with me?"

"Of course! It's stunning. It's magnificent. You must realize that. You must realize the work and talent and creativity that went into it. Any girl would want to share that. Maybe if you brought your ex-girlfriend up there, she would have moved into it with you and you never would have had to break up with her."

"No, I don't think so. I thought of that when I was trying to decide whether to stay with her. I considered bringing her up to the cabin and showing it to her and maybe asking her to move in there with me, but I didn't."

"Why not?" She rests her chin in her hand again and studies me with unwavering attention while we talk, but she doesn't scowl at me and her gaze radiates warmth and connection and gladness that we're talking. She doesn't burn with buried resentment and haunted demons anymore. "Why didn't you give her that chance?"

"I guess that's what I'm saying. I loved her, but I didn't realize until then that I didn't want to live with her in either place. I would have brought her to my cabin long before then if I did want that. I would have shared that with her instead of trying to keep it all to myself."

"Do you regret having me there? I didn't mean to intrude on your privacy by showing up on your doorstep."

"No, I don't feel that way about you." I find myself captivated by the intense depth of her eyes. She's never looked at me like this. I hardly recognize her as the same person.

Her eyes dart sideways and she leans just a little bit closer. "Would you want to share it with me....if it went that far?"

"Of course. I would want to share everything with you. That's why I would want to rebuild my dad's house—in case the cabin wasn't big enough."

Her eyes pop and all the color drains from her face now that she understands what I'm saying. Her biological clock is ticking. She wants to find someone she can build a future with.

Things would only go in one direction if they went anywhere between us. They would go toward us needing a bigger house. The cabin wouldn't be big enough for that.

"Maybe I feel that way about everything." I glance at my phone and put it back in my pocket. "Maybe I've never done anything with my life because I never had a reason to....until now."

"What would you do if you had a reason to?"

"I don't know. I would have to think about it and figure it out. I've never had to think about it before. Nothing has ever given me a reason to break out of this little hamster wheel I've been running around on. It's been a lucrative hamster wheel, but it's still a hamster wheel."

She bursts out laughing again, but at that moment, a crash startles both of us from behind. We both spin around to see Anita standing at the counter. She glares at both of us with the same disgusted expression. She must have dropped something to get our attention.

"I think your chaperone is trying to tell you something," I mutter.

Jordan laughs again. "Don't mind her. I'll deal with her later."

"How will you do that?"

"I'll give her a stern talking-to. I'll give her some tough love, although I did that already after she busted us at the park. If she can't pull her head in, we're going to have a problem."

"Are you sure you want to alienate your best friend...over me?"

She beams at me and then, like something out of a dream, she extends her hand and squeezes my arm where it's resting on the chair. "She won't be my best friend if she has a problem with me going out with you."

I frown at her even more. "What is going on with you? Why are you acting so nice to me all of a sudden?"

"Because I realize that I want to go out with you. I had a little mental switch after I went home from your place yesterday and I realized that I was just throwing obstacles in my own path. I wanted to go out with you before, but for some reason, I didn't let myself."

"That probably had something to do with the way you remembered me from high school."

She shrugs again. "Maybe. Anyway, it doesn't matter because you aren't that person. You're you and I want to go out with you. I guess that's why I kept trying to hook up with you without ever letting my guard down....but it doesn't matter now. I'm over it....so when do you want to go out?"

"It's Friday. We could go out tonight."

She bursts with sunshine again. "Great! I can't wait."

I furrow my brow trying to figure her out. I keep waiting for her intense, scowling fury to come back, but it doesn't. Is she going to be like this from now on?

She nods toward the door. "If you aren't trading, do you want to go for a walk or something?"

"Okay." I stand up and we both head for the door.

She walks out first and beams at me while she holds the door open for me to follow her. As soon as we both get out on the sidewalk, she takes my hand and squeezes. She won't stop smiling at me.

I can just feel Anita glaring at us as we walk away, but Jordan doesn't even glance at her friend. I can just imagine how things are going to go between them when Jordan gives Anita a talking-to about me.

My heart soars, now that I'm walking down the street holding hands with Jordan. "Where do you park your truck when you come to the coffee shop each morning?" she asks.

"I don't drive. I walk."

She whips around and gasps. "You walk—from your house?"

"Yeah. I enjoy walking in the mountains early in the morning. It makes me happy and puts me in the right mental state before I start trading."

She blinks at me and then shakes her head before she starts walking again. "That's incredible. You must have to leave really early in the morning."

"I leave at four AM and I get here at nine—just in time for the market to open. It works out pretty well and then I can stop by the overlook on my way home. It makes for a nice workday."

She gapes at me in amazement, but she doesn't drill me with her fierce stare. She just takes it all in like she's just now realizing what a gem I am. Wow. Whatever happened to change her mind must have been huge.

Not that I'm complaining. If this new and improved Jordan is the woman I'm going to be going out with tonight, then this could be the most game-changing date of my life. I was just thinking yesterday that the world better look out if I ever made her smile for real.

I don't know if I'm the one who made her smile like this, but I'll just have to get on board the rollercoaster and hold on for dear life. She's taking me there whether I'm ready for it or not.

I'm ready for it. I'm ready for anything and anywhere she wants to go. She's worth it. I got an inkling of it before. Now I'm certain of it.

We stop at an intersection while we wait for the signal to cross. "Can I give you a ride home?" she asks.

The blood rushes to my cheeks. "You're really taking this role-reversal thing to the limit."

She laughs right out loud again. Her eyes sparkle and her whole face lights up. "I won't do it anymore if it bothers you. I just thought, if you don't have a car and we have a date tonight, you might need to get home sooner than usual. I guess we haven't even discussed when you're going to pick me up."

"I can pick you up whenever you want me to."

"How about eight?"

"Okay. Perfect."

"Does that give you enough time to walk home? Do you do extra work at the overlook? I really didn't mean to mess up your whole routine."

"You didn't. I'm always happy to spend time with you and I don't need to trade every day."

"So....do you want to walk home or catch a ride with me?"

"I'll catch a ride with you if you're driving."

She splits in another grin. Damn, she looks incredibly happy.

She steers me toward the parking lot behind the coffee shop and she bursts out laughing when she opens the passenger door for me.

I get in and she gets behind the wheel. "Do you need to make any stops in town before you go home?" she asks.

"No."

She bites her lips to stop herself from grinning, but this is totally different from yesterday. Her features can't contain her happiness and delight at my company. I really don't know what to make of her.

She drives out of town. "My address is 296 Saddle Mountain Road, just so you know."

"Thanks."

She shoots me glances while she drives. "Are you okay?"

"You're making me nervous. I've never seen you this happy."

She laughs. "Sorry."

"You don't have to be sorry. I just keep expecting you to switch back to the way you were yesterday. I can't think of any reason why you would suddenly change so drastically."

"Let's just say that making the decision to go out with you makes me happy."

"I suppose I should be happy about that, too."

"Yes, you should." She laughs at my expression. "When you come over to pick me up, I'd like you to come inside and meet my dad."

"The cop? Great," I mutter. "Is he going to meet me at the door with a loaded shotgun?"

"No, nothing like that. He just cares about me a lot and I know he'd like to meet you before we go out."

"Does he approve all of your dates? I'm sure he would rather see you going out with Holden than me."

"He doesn't approve my dates and he didn't say anything about it. I'm the one who wants you to meet him."

"Whatever you say."

"Can I ask you a question?" she asks.

"Sure. Go ahead."

"Did you recognize my dad when he drove me up to the overlook? Do you know any of the cops in this town?"

"No, I don't know any of them. I don't know if I had a record before I lost my memory, but I haven't had anything to do with any cop since then."

"So you didn't recognize my dad at the overlook?"

"No. Why?"

"I'm just curious."

"Did he recognize me? Did he bust me or something back in my deep, dark past?"

"He wouldn't tell me, but if he did bust you, I doubt he would let you know it. You mentioned that Frankie and Dr. Patterson know about your memory loss. I would bet you anything my dad knows about it, too. He won't hold anything against you. I'm certain of it."

"I hope you're right."

"I am. He's a good guy. I think you two will like each other."

"What makes you think that? He's a cop. How could we have anything in common?"

"You have me in common." She pulls into the driveway and parks in front of my dad's house. "Here we are. I can't wait to see you tonight."

"Do you want to come inside for a while?"

"I'd love to, but......" She bends in and kisses me deeply and passionately. Her wicked little hand slips over my thigh and gives me a rush of hot desire. "If I did that, we'd probably never leave and we wouldn't wind up going out on a date at all."

"You're right." I sink deeper into her kiss, and when she squeezes my thigh just a few inches higher, I let my hand migrate to her breast.

She moans and her breath catches when I massage her breast through her bra. Fuck, she is so damn hot! She wants it right now and she leans closer to me.

I take a chance, thread my fingers into her hair, and kiss her wildly while I slide my other hand up between her legs to her crotch. She whines and then spasms when I start rubbing her. She rocks in her seat and her hand closes over my swelling fly.

I drag her closer to me rubbing her harder and faster. Her breath quickens along with the panting, desperate sobs of rising lust and hunger. I could drag her inside and nail her to the wall again. I could bend her over my bed and take her to the stars.

She would love it if I did, but just when I think about getting out of the car and leading her up to the cabin, she straightens up and takes hold of my wrist.

She breathes fast and hard and her drunken eyes float open in front of me. She keeps kissing me while she fights herself under control. "Later...." she breathes. "Tonight...."

"Is that what this is about?" I ask. "You want to do it tonight?"

"I want to do it now, but I want to go out on a date with you first. I want to do this the right way."

"Is there a wrong way?"

She laughs and then breaks off in a ragged moan when I push my hand between her legs again. She's wearing jeans so I can't reach her without tearing all her clothes off.

"You want me, don't you, baby?" I growl. "You want me in there...."

"Please.... Rafe...."

"Come up to my house, baby," I murmur. "I need you now."

"Later...." She gives me a long, succulent kiss and pulls away. "Tonight."

"You promise?"

She blushes and grins. "If you still want to."

"Of course I'll want to."

She kisses me one more time. "I'll see you at eight at my house."

That's my cue. I steal one last kiss and get out of the car. She waves to me with her cheeks still glowing with pleasure, reverses out of the driveway, and drives off down the mountain.

Chapter 13: Jordan

I study myself in my bedroom mirror, smooth down my dress, and check my hair. I'm wearing the same sparkly, navy-blue dress I wore on my date with Holden, but that doesn't matter. I only have so many nice dresses and Rafe won't care.

I head downstairs at ten minutes to eight and find Anita in the kitchen with my parents. "I'm on my way out," I tell them.

"Congratulations, sweetie." My dad kisses me on the forehead. "I'm happy for you."

"Thanks, Dad."

"Do you really think it's a good idea to go out with Rafe Mendoza?" my mom asks. "You know what people say about him."

"I know all about what people say about him, Mom, and I wouldn't be going out with him if I didn't think it was a good idea. You've been listening to Anita too much."

"Don't waste your breath trying to convince her," Anita tells my mom. "She's got a thing for him."

"What thing?" my mom asks.

"Look, you two stay in here and talk about my thing all night if you want to. Don't go out there when Rafe is here. I don't want you anywhere near him until you change your attitude."

"As if that's likely to happen," Anita mutters.

I walk out and go into the front hall. I'm checking that I have everything in my handbag when I hear Rafe's truck pull into the driveway. He's almost ten minutes early.

He springs up the steps and I open the door for him. He's wearing a plain blue suit with no tie and brown leather shoes that look like they've been around for a while.

He smiles at me and I smile back. "Are you ready to go?" he asks.

"Yeah. I'm ready."

Just then, my dad comes out of the kitchen. He's alone, thank the stars. He smiles back and forth between me and Rafe. "Heading out?"

"Yeah. We'll be going now." I wave between him and Rafe. "Rafe Mendoza, this is my dad, Isaac Cruz."

My dad extends a hand to Rafe. His smile is much warmer than the condescending one he bestowed on Holden. "Good to meet you, son."

"Yes, Sir. It's good to meet you, too."

I kiss my dad on the cheek. "I love you, Dad."

"Have a nice time. Drive safely, son."

"I will, Sir."

I step out onto the porch, pull the door shut, and take Rafe's hand.

"He was really nice," Rafe murmurs.

"I told you. He's a nice guy. You won't have any problem with him."

We walk over to Rafe's truck. The passenger door creaks loudly when he pries it open and the seat groans when I sit on the old springs. The upholstery looks like it's about forty years out of date and the door clangs when he slams it shut.

I pull on my seatbelt while he gets behind the wheel and bangs his door shut even more loudly. This truck is a dinosaur, but that only makes this whole experience so much more appealing.

I love that Rafe doesn't care about appearances. He's so different from Holden. Rafe never lets anything external get in the way of our connection, whether that external is his vast wealth or his junky truck, his used clothes, or anything else. This date and every other moment I've shared with him is just him and me with nothing in between.

The motor grinds when he turns the ignition and the truck creaks down the driveway. Rafe glances over at me when he eases out onto the mountain road. His eyes catch me in their overpowering hypnotic sway and I stretch out my hand to take his.

He grabs my hand and steers with his left. We hold hands driving down the mountain. "So where are we going?" I ask.

"You went to Ravenwood Estates with Holden, so I thought we'd do something a little different."

"What did you have in mind?"

"You'll see. I'll show you when we get there, but I can promise it won't be anything like Ravenwood Estates."

"That's good."

He cocks his head to study me before going back to looking at the road. "Why didn't you like it there? It's supposed to be really nice."

"It is really nice. I guess it was just the company. Everything he does is fake and the restaurant being really nice was just another part of that."

"I probably would have taken you there if you didn't tell me not to."

"Really? Why would you take me there of all places?"

"Because I would want to give you the best. All this time, I've just been waiting for something to come along that really grabbed me and made me think it was worth spending my money on, but nothing ever has grabbed me that way. I keep looking at all these cars and phones and planes and clothes and I keep thinking none of them is worth the money. I don't feel that way about you. I probably would have bought a different car just for this date if you hadn't sprung it on me at such short notice."

I have to beam at him and I squeeze his hand. "You don't have to do that. You don't have to be anything you aren't. I'm going out with you because I like you the way you are."

He meets my eye and compresses my hand back. "I like you the way you are, too."

"Tell the truth. You like me better this way than I was when we first met."

"I liked you then, too. I liked that you were genuine. You showed me who you really were and didn't try to pretend to like me."

"I liked you. I pretended not to."

"Even better."

He pulls off the road and I frown at the surroundings. "What are we doing here?"

"This is where we're going on our date. Do you like it?"

I can't stop staring through the windshield as he pulls into another rest stop. It isn't the Desolation Heights overlook, but it's another lookout point where we can see a broad sweeping view of the mountains.

The moon shines over everything and a river of stars lights up the sky. It's a perfect night, except that we're in the middle of nowhere.

He gets out, opens my door for me, and takes my hand. "Come on. It's all set up."

I don't know what to think until he leads me to the edge of the ridge. He climbs over the guard rail and walks out onto a flat rock like the one at the overlook.

He pulls me down on a blanket spread over the rock. Two Coleman lanterns cast the blanket in pale golden light. A large cooler sits there along with a picnic basket and an enormous suitcase. "What is this all about?" I ask.

"We're on a date." He sits down opposite me and opens the cooler.

He pulls out a bottle of chilled white wine and then takes two wine glasses from the picnic basket. He pours a glass for each of us and starts unpacking the rest of the basket.

He takes out plates, cutlery, and two cloth napkins. He sets up the blanket like a tablecloth and then starts taking food out of the cooler.

"This is awesome," I breathe. "Did you set this up today?"

"Of course. I don't leave all this lying around just in case some girl ambushes me at the Daily Grind and asks me out."

I can't help studying him when he takes a plastic container of salad, a crusty loaf of sourdough bread, and a container of butter out of the cooler. He cuts the bread with a knife out of the basket, butters the slices, and puts them on both of our plates before he serves us both salad.

He finally sits back, raises his wine glass, and sips it. "So here we are."

"This is the best date I've ever been on," I tell him.

"I'm flattered. It isn't the Ravenwood Estates, but it is pretty nice. You can't see the stars from inside a restaurant."

I gaze at the view while I sip my wine. "Do you come here often?"

He bursts out laughing. "You're supposed to save that line for picking up creepy guys at bars."

"I just meant do you always go to Desolation Heights? Do you ever go to any other rest stop?"

"No, it's always Desolation Heights. I love that place. I only brought you here because I didn't think you'd want to go there on a date."

"I wouldn't mind. I don't feel the same way about it as I did when I met you. Getting to know you makes it mean something different. It doesn't upset me anymore because it means you, not the accident."

"I'm glad I could give you that." He takes my hand again and we hold hands while we sip our wine.

I take a deep breath. "I need to tell you something."

"Okay. I'm listening."

"The accident....caused a lot of damage to my body. I got thrown out of the car and I have a lot of scars on my stomach and chest and legs."

He frowns at me. "Really? I guess I didn't get a chance to see those when you came over to my place."

"Right. I just want you to know so you don't get surprised if we ever do it again and you see them."

He raises his eyebrows. "*If* we ever do it again? You promised we would do it again tonight."

"I just want to leave the door open. The scars are pretty bad and they've gotten worse since the accident. The scar tissue keeps getting thicker and more noticeable. I considered getting plastic surgery to reduce them, but the doctors say that it might just come back. It could keep coming back for the rest of my life."

"Why would that stop me from doing it with you?"

I shrug. "You wouldn't be the first guy who has decided not to."

His eyes bug out of their sockets. "Are you telling me that guys have decided not to do it with you because of that? Jesus!"

"It isn't just that. Sometimes I'll get to know a guy and it becomes obvious that he isn't going to accept it....... or maybe that I just don't want to go there with him in that way.....like Holden. I realize pretty early on that I don't want to take the chance of exposing something as.....I don't want to call it shameful, but it isn't easy for me to show somebody something that makes me look bad. If I think a guy isn't going to accept it, I just don't let it go that far. Maybe they would accept it and I just don't want to take the chance. I don't know."

He leans over and kisses me. "You could be disfigured from the neck down and never look bad. Nothing could make you look bad and you have nothing to be ashamed of. If you showed it to me, I would accept it. If we were going to go there, it would be because of who you are, not because of your scars."

"I know that. I knew you would say that. That's why I'm telling you. Most of the time, I don't even tell them that I have the scars."

He puts his glass down, takes his hand away from mine, and starts unzipping the suitcase. "Now I understand why you haven't been able to make it work with anybody."

He distracts me by getting busy taking stuff out of his suitcase. "What are you doing?"

"We're having dinner."

He opens the suitcase and takes out a large bundle wrapped in a towel. Several lengths of twine hold the towel in place and he cuts the twine with a pair of scissors.

He unwinds the towel to reveal a ceramic casserole dish inside. He uses the towel to take off the lid and succulent steam billows from inside.

He pulls a spoon out of the picnic basket, lifts my plate, and starts serving me big spoonfuls of roast pork so tender it falls apart when he touches it. He piles my plate with meat, roasted potatoes, and vegetables steamed in the dish.

"How did you do all this?" I ask when he puts my plate in front of me.

"Let's just say it's a good thing you gave me a ride home from town or I wouldn't have had time to set this up for tonight. You didn't want to go to Ravenwood Estates, so I had to come up with the next best thing."

I don't know what to say. The food is beyond tempting. It smells better than anything my mom has ever made and it doesn't disappoint when I put a piece of the meat in my mouth.

"How did you learn to cook?"

"We had to learn in rehab, and then, when I came home, I had to cook for my dad. His health started to fail almost as soon as I came home, so I had to take care of everything for him."

"That sounds hard."

"It was, but it was good for me, too. It forced me to learn how to function again. I had to learn how to keep the house clean—or relatively clean. I had to learn how to manage both of our lives. It was a learning experience, but it helped me get back on my feet."

"Did you do anything like this with your ex-girlfriend?"

"No, nothing like this." He gazes across the shadowy landscape. "She was a city girl. She liked doing things in the city."

I find myself studying him again. He loves the mountains so much. No wonder he didn't want to leave and no wonder he never asked her to come and live in the mountains. She wouldn't have been happy here.

I follow his gaze to the peaks and valleys vanishing into the distance. Would I be happy to spend the rest of my life here? Would I be content to stay in Oak Falls for the rest of my life?

I've never let myself ask those questions. I've never let myself see beyond the immediate problem of letting my guard down around people.

"What are you thinking about?" he asks.

"Just.... everything—what I'm doing with my life."

"That's probably going to be something you need to think about for a while—forever, maybe."

"You're right. I don't know why I expect myself to have all the answers."

"You aren't eating your food."

I jump a foot in the air and bend over my plate. "Sorry. It's delicious."

"I'm glad you like it."

I almost ask if he's going to cook like this all the time when we're....I don't ask that, though. I'm not ready to start thinking like that.

"You mentioned that your relationship with your dad never went back to the way it was before the accident," I continue. "What happened?"

"I don't know what our relationship was like before the accident, but he never let me forget that I was different. It really upset him. He kept saying that he lost his son when I lost my memory. He said his son died and left a stranger in his place. My dad cried about it a lot toward the end."

"Wow," I breathe. "That's terrible."

"It was terrible for him. I had no frame of reference for it. My whole family was a bunch of strangers to me. I was surrounded by strangers and I never felt any differently about him the longer I spent around him. I never loved him, which I guess just made it so much worse for him. He could see that I was treating him like a stranger, which he was.

It tore his heart out which led to him giving up and letting his health go even more. It wasn't pretty."

"I'm so sorry you had to go through that." I want to touch him. I raise my hand and wind up stroking his cheek.

Everything that he's been through draws me to him more powerfully than before. He's been through so much—even more than I have.

He gazes back into my eyes and we both lean in and start kissing.

Chapter 14: Rafe

J ordan slides across the blanket kissing me long and deep, but she doesn't tear into me like a wild animal the way she did before. She savors my lips with slow, succulent kisses that make me ache for her.

I put my arm around her waist, but that doesn't bring us close enough. She turns toward me and winds up climbing onto my lap. She straddles me on the rock and hugs her body tight against me.

I can't stop touching and caressing every part of her, but this deep desire for her goes so far beyond wanting to tear her clothes off and ravage her body. I almost don't want it to go any further than just this steady, easy, mind-blowing kissing.

I want to enjoy every luscious twirl of her tongue and the soft pulse of her body moving with mine. She doesn't seem in too big a hurry to speed things along, either.

I stroke up her spine and her hair tumbles over me when she leans into my arms. Her eyes flash in the lantern light. I couldn't have come up with a more romantic place to take her on a date. I'm a genius.

I squeeze her waist and migrate up to her breasts. She moans when I squeeze them and a shudder of ecstasy goes through her body. She can feel me getting hard underneath her.

"Do you want to come home with me, baby?" I whisper.

She gulps and nods before her eyelids float open. That intoxicated hunger in her gaze makes my guts clench. I want so, so much of her. I can't get enough. I don't even have the heart to move her off me so we can both get up.

I would do it with her right here, but something tells me not to. I glide my hands down her sides and pull her hips against me. I drill into her from below and she moans again when she rocks on my stiff bulge.

Not even that can break the spell between us. I don't even need to take her clothes off. Just having her here with me is too perfect. This whole date is exactly what I dreamed it would be. I would still think it's perfect if she asked me to take her back to her parents' place right now.

She leans back and looks into my eyes. "Was this part of your plan?"

"Absolutely. See? Look."

I pull open the suitcase to show her a stack of blankets. She bursts out laughing. "Did you bring a tent?"

"No, that would be too cheesy. Doing it in a tent in the middle of the wilderness—it's the cheesiest cliché ever."

She laughs again. "I didn't think of that."

"Let me guess. This isn't what you had in mind when you said we'd do it later tonight."

"No. It isn't." Her eyes communicate so many hidden meanings. I know she didn't mean that and she didn't want to do it on a rock, either.

"Did you get enough to eat?" I ask.

She nods. "Did you?"

"Yes. I'm not hungry anymore.... not for food, at least."

She blushes. I love making her smile like that. She knows exactly what I mean.

"Let's get out of here," I tell her. "I'm sure we can find somewhere more comfortable to spend the rest of our evening."

She stands up and I start packing up the picnic basket, the suitcase, and the cooler. She takes the lanterns off the blanket and folds it up. Then she helps me carry everything back to my truck.

We keep shooting each other knowing grins until we go back to the rock, pick up a lantern each, and carry them back to the road.

I blow them out and pack them in the back before opening her door for her. She slides in, but before I close it, I move in for another deep kiss. Her hands grab me and she pulls me in. Her old passion bursts back to life and she starts clawing at me.

I want to attack her, but I can't reach much of her when she's sitting on the seat and I'm standing outside it. I slide my hand up her dress and she whimpers when I touch her saturated panties. I love that about her. She always wants me and every obstacle only turns her on more.

I maul her mouth kissing her faster. She leans back in the seat and I end up sticking my whole upper body into the cab to reach her. I can't stop pinching her breasts and driving my fingers into her dripping channel. God damn, I need to take her right now.

Her hand glides between my legs and I practically explode when she starts stroking me through my pants. She can feel how hard I am and she loves it. She seizes me in her hot little fist and crushes me until I gasp.

She keeps pumping her hips against my hand and her juices gush all over the seat. She pants and whines in my mouth rising to screams. Oh, fuck, yes.

I break off her mouth and gnaw down her neck to her chest, but I can't reach her breasts without taking her dress off right here.

She bursts into full whining cries now that my mouth isn't there to muffle her. She arches back riding my hand and shoving her chest into my face. She hugs my head tight and spreads her thighs for me to finger her.

Her wicked squeezes drive me out of my mind. I need to get her home or I'll have no choice but to bend her over the seat right now.

I straighten up and her bleary eyes give me another surge of adrenaline. She's already blurry with desire. I have to have her.

I break away and go around to the driver's seat. She rubs my arm when I get in and she won't stop touching me while I start the motor and pull out onto the road.

She slides across the truck seat and wraps her arms around me. She kisses the side of my neck, nibbles my ears, and nuzzles into my hair while I drive. Her hands and arms keep winding around me, touching every part of me, and distracting me from the road. I have to concentrate hard not to attack her.

She slips her hands inside my jacket, but thank God she stops short of pulling up my shirt. I couldn't drive if she touched my skin. She does massage my thighs, though she stays away from my junk.

I hold it together just long enough to get back to my place. The instant I park the truck, I turn to kiss her and it's all on. She rips at my shirt pulling it out of my belt and her hand closes on my shaft.

I try to get a hold of her, but she's too ravenous to let me near her. She tugs my shirt up, and as soon as she lays her hand on my stomach, she dives under my arms, burrows under my shirt, and starts kissing my chest and sides.

The first kiss explodes me out of my mind and I collapse back in the seat gasping for air. Holy fuck, her mouth feels like molten lava. She nips me working her way up to my chest and around to my shoulders.

Every kiss sets me on fire, and then, incredibly, she moves down to my belt. Her hand slithers between my thighs and she starts manhandling me while she pulls my belt off with her teeth.

I don't want to let this happen. I need to take her inside, but she's already moving her head down to my crotch and biting me through my pants. I groan in agony as she slides my zipper down. Holy shit. This is not happening. She isn't doing this to me.

I grab the steering wheel trying desperately to hold it all together, but every hot breath seeping through my pants sends me reeling into a state of dizzy ecstasy. She shifts onto her knees on the floor and then I'm in her mouth.

I contort on the seat as she starts to suck. Her mouth feels unbelievably hot and wet and brutally inviting. She'll suck me dry in a second if she isn't careful, but she doesn't seem too concerned about that.

She lashes her tongue around me and I moan in desperate need. I try to throw myself back in the seat, but I can't go anywhere. She pins me in place with that masterful mouth of hers.

Her hands crawl up my stomach and she caresses my chest while she drives me insane with her mouth. I can't take this for much longer.

I try to pull her off, but I wind up rubbing the back of her neck as her scorching hot lips drag up my shaft and she swallows me down her throat.

"Baby...." I choke. "Baby.... please.....I want you....."

She doesn't stop. She clamps down even harder and makes me sob as my world comes crashing down around my ears.

"Please.... baby....come inside.....with me......please......I want you...inside...."

She finally sits back on her heels and studies me while I pant and grimace trying to haul myself back from the brink. Her hands on my chest and midsection don't make it any easier.

"Do you like that?" she whispers.

"Baby.... you're killing me...."

She climbs onto the seat and her mouth meets mine. She straddles me in front of the steering wheel and sits her soaking wet panties right on top of me.

"Baby...." I mumble between kisses. "Baby.... come inside......I don't want to do it like this......"

She kisses me a few more times and then leans back to look at me. Fuck, she looks wild! What am I going to do with this girl?

She eases off onto the seat, straightens her dress, and turns away. She waits while I zip up, get out of the truck, and open her door for her.

Her hand slips into mine and we walk up to the cabin in silence. I wouldn't put it past her to tackle me the minute we get inside, but she doesn't.

I put my keys and wallet on the kitchen counter, but she just stands there looking around my cabin like she's never seen it before. She clutches my hand and hovers close to my side. For a girl who was just going at me like a banshee a few minutes ago, she's sure acting uncertain now.

I lead her toward the stairs and up to my room. I don't turn on the light until we get there, and when I do, she looks around at the room, too. She doesn't know what to do.

I take off my jacket, lay it on the chair by the bed, and then go over to her. Her eyes don't light up with mischief or even ravenous lust. She looks scared.

I cradle her cheeks and kiss her, but that pained expression only gets worse with every passing second. She puts her arms around me and I feel her shaking.

I hug her head into my chest. I don't want to attack her when she's like this. I just want to make it easier for her, but when I gaze down into those eyes, I see that nothing will make it easier.

"Are you sure about this?" I whisper.

She gulps and nods. Her nostrils flare when she tries to breathe. Her hands feel cold when I squeeze them.

I back away toward the dresser so she stands between me and the bed. She squirms in front of me, rubs her arms, and tries to look around. She shifts her weight from one leg to the other in an agony of uncertainty.

I straighten up and level her with a direct, unbending stare. "Take your clothes off for me, baby."

She twists a few more times and then lowers her eyes to the floor. She won't look at me while she slides down the zipper of her dress. She can reach the spot between her shoulder blades easily and she wriggles her hips slithering out of the dress.

She drops it on the floor and I see the scars on her stomach. They're as ugly and knobbled and puffy as she said. They slash up her ribs and snake down her milk-white thighs.

She unhooks her bra and drops it on top of her dress. Then she pushes down her panties, discards them, and steps out of her shoes to stand flat on the floor.

She stands before me naked and raw and so, so beautiful. Every flicker of emotion crossing her face makes her so impossibly beautiful that it hurts to look at her.

She keeps her eyes down until she takes all her clothes off just like I asked. Then, when she stands before me completely naked, she squares her shoulders, throws back her head, shakes her hair out of her eyes, and locks her eyes on me in a ferocious glare of challenge.

That look makes her so impossibly beautiful that I can't keep away from her. I want her more than ever—not because of her scars but because she's so defiant about them. She challenges me to accept her in every detail.

I want to do so much more than accept her. I want to love her. I want to worship her. I want to cherish her and nurture her and watch her flourish.

I saunter over to her and I can't even see her scars anymore. That fierce lick of flame in her eyes consumes me. This is what I want. I want her facing me and demanding that I be the man she needs me to be. I need to be that man to her.

I stand before her as exposed as she is—probably more so. She never lets me get away with anything. She always challenges me to be more. I need to be more. I need to love her with every particle of my being.

I cup her beautiful cheeks and kiss her. She kisses me back and puts her arms around my neck to lay her magnificent body against me. She doesn't hold back from me. She wants me as much now as she did in the truck.

There's something I need to do first, though. I slip my fingers into her hair, clench into a fist, and pull her head back. I dive into her neck kissing down to her collarbone.

I work my way lower to her breasts and she sobs in delight when I kiss and suck and nibble them. She combs her fingers through my hair and pushes her body at me the way she did before, but that isn't what I want.

I fall on my knees in front of her, slip my arms around her waist, and kiss the scars all over her stomach and sides and hips. She keeps raking her fingers through my hair and sighing. She doesn't try to stop me or make me hurry up.

I could worship these scars forever. They mean so much to me, now that I know I'm the only man who has ever done this. This is all mine. These scars are mine to love and they break my heart in half with love for her. I'll do anything to keep this feeling in my life. I never want to lose this.

Chapter 15: Jordan

I close my eyes feeling the overwhelming flood of emotion as Rafe presses his lips to my scars. I knew he would accept them. I just never thought it would mean this much.

He wraps his arms around my waist and drags his face and lips and eyes across my stomach. Every breath rasps with love and desire. I don't have to hide from the realization that he loves me. He loves everything about me, even this—especially this.

I run my fingers through his hair and sway in the swell of mind-blowing emotion, but it isn't shame or fear or revulsion that someone is seeing my scars and touching them and making a big deal about them.

I just feel happy—and relieved. It's over. I don't have to worry anymore about someone seeing them or how he'll react.

He lets out another deep, satisfied sigh. "You are so beautiful, baby!" he whispers into my stomach. "This is mine. This is all mine."

I swallow hard feeling his fingertips flex against my back as he pulls me into his mouth. He wants this. He wants me like this. He wants to be the one kissing me and loving me and showing me how beautiful I am.

My heart aches with love for him. I love him. I don't have to hide from that, either. How could I not love someone who acts this way?

He stands up and his eyes occupy my whole awareness. I drown in that look that tells me he sees me and knows me for everything that I am. He knows everything about me and he wants me. He does more than want me. He worships me.

He kisses me a few times and then nods toward the bed. "Lie down where I can see you, baby. I want to see how beautiful you are."

I sit down on the bed and then crawl back to lie down. I stretch out and relax where he can see me. The lamp by the bed shines down my body and he stands over me surveying me from the top of my head to the tips of my toes.

I gaze back up at him letting this tempest of emotion wash over me. I would never let anyone see me like this before tonight, but that only confirms that I was right about him. His gaze makes me something totally different. I might even be a different person just because he's looking at me like this. His gaze changes me.

He stands there examining every inch of me. He doesn't move for a long time, and when he does, he doesn't take his clothes off or try to take me.

He sits down on the edge of the bed. He doesn't try to stop me from touching him, but he doesn't move any closer. He just sits there staring at me.

He raises his hand with impossible slowness and drags it up my side. He lets his fingertips trail around my nipple and watches me tremble and moan and shudder at the powerful waves of sensation coursing through me.

He glides up my neck to stroke my cheek and then migrates down my sternum to my stomach. He passes his warm, soft palm over my scars and then down to my thighs.

He grazes his fingers up between my thighs, barely brushes my swollen slit, and goes back to stroking the rest of my body.

He observes and admires the torturous whines and sobs shaking me all over as he touches me, but he doesn't try to escalate. He doesn't stop me from squeezing his arms or raking my fingernails at his shirt or touching his face, but those insistent signals don't affect him.

He caresses down my sides, covers my scars with his comforting touch, and then moves back down to my thighs. He rubs me between my legs until I twitch and spasm in front of him, but he always leaves me hungry for more.

"You are so fucking beautiful, baby," he whispers. "You have no idea how beautiful you are."

I feel beautiful when he touches me and looks at me like that. Why did I think my scars somehow made me repulsive to anyone? He must have been right. I just hadn't found the right guy yet.

He brushes my breasts again and hesitates there just long enough to squeeze my nipple between the flat edges of his fingers. I moan and contort at his touch, but he just moves on.

I try to pull him nearer, but he won't budge. He's enjoying himself too much. He wants to give me this. He wants me to understand how beautiful I am to him. His eyes tell me all I need to know.

He keeps looking down at my body shivering and spasming with desire. He takes in my breasts, my thighs, my hips, my scars, my face, my arms—it's all the same to him. No part of me is less beautiful than any other part.

"Please......" I rasp. "Please.... kiss me......"

He bends down and kisses me. I grab him and try to pull him down. I want him more than ever, now that I know I don't have to worry about him finding out anything shameful about me.

Once he starts kissing me, I can't let him go. I pull him down on top of me snatching at his shirt and trying to reach his belt. He sinks into my mouth kissing me back.

I wrap my legs around him, tug his shirt up, and he doesn't stop me from taking it off. My desire explodes off the charts once I get it off. I want to feel every inch of his skin. I want his body naked and touching mine. I don't want any space or daylight between him and me.

I thread my arms around his ribs and he groans when I kiss his chest. God, I love the sounds he makes when I touch him. I try to crawl down to his stomach, but he won't let me. He catches my lips and makes me kiss him while my body flies into a frenzy trying to reach him.

He pivots onto his hands and knees above me. His muscular arms and chest give me all the real estate I need to feel how strong and sturdy he is, but that isn't enough.

His eyes pop wide open when I take hold of his belt. I can already feel how hard he is. I want him in my mouth and everywhere else.

He studies me while I unbuckle his belt and slide down his zipper. I weasel my hand into his shorts and his eyes slip out of focus when I take hold of him.

I try to keep kissing him while I stroke him, but his lips freeze. He gasps and groans in my mouth as his rod throbs in my hand. Man, he feels so good like this!

His eyes watch my every move when I ease his pants down and he kicks them off. He lowers himself on top of me and now his skin is touching me all over. I can feel every particle of his magnificent being touching every part of me. His stomach touches my stomach and my breasts crush into his chest.

He lies there hard and ready between my legs, but he doesn't do anything except undulate against me in slow, gentle, sensual waves. He kisses me and gazes into my eyes as we both gauge this earth-shattering moment.

I hug my legs around his waist, but I don't need to accomplish anything anymore. I can just lie here and appreciate the majesty of this moment. It's everything I ever wanted.

His body vibrates with desire and I know he feels the same from me. Little by little, this subtle rippling energy pulsating between us builds higher until it won't be denied any longer.

He flexes his hips and he's in. He fills me full of his powerful masculine strength and I dissolve in such a blissful flood of rapture that I can't help but sigh. He carries me out of my world to somewhere beyond everything I've ever known.

He rises on his elbows looking down at me while we kiss and flow together. His eyes ask me all the questions that can't get through his lips while we're kissing.

He doesn't need to see my scars because he already knows they're there. Only we matter now—this glorious understanding that surpasses words and questions and everything else.

Chapter 16: Rafe

I wake up early in the morning the way I always do. I've been waking up early for so long that I wind up waking up at the same time whether I need to go to town or not.

Jordan fell asleep with her head on my chest and her arms around me, but she must have rolled away in her sleep. She lies with her back to me now so I can slip out of bed without waking her up.

I tiptoe downstairs and out of the cabin. Mist shrouds the mountains and everything is quiet and peaceful. It feels strange not to have to walk into town the way I usually do. I don't know what to do with myself without that.

I'm going to need to figure it out, now that I have Jordan. My life is going to change after this. I just don't know how.

I get the stuff out of the back of the truck and bring it up to the porch, but I don't go back inside. I don't want the noise to bother her.

I wander around for a while and end up studying the wreck of my dad's old house. I could rebuild it in a few weeks if I hired a construction team to do it. Is that what I want?

I might decide to do something different. Jordan might not want to live here. Then what? I might wind up moving to the city after all. What would be the point of rebuilding this house if I'm going to do that—if *we're* going to do that?

Then there's the question of whether we would want to live here if we had a family. Would I want my kids going to Oak Falls High School? Would Jordan? This isn't exactly a thriving center of educational opportunity. Kids could do a lot better somewhere else.

I don't know why I'm even thinking that. Jordan and I have gone on one date. We haven't committed to staying together forever or even staying together at all. Maybe she doesn't want that. Maybe she just wanted to know that someone would accept her the way she is. Maybe I'm not what she wants. Why would I be?

The sun starts peeking over the nearest mountain when the cabin door opens. She steps out wrapped in a blanket. Her hair is a mess, but she never looked more beautiful.

She comes over to me and kisses me. "There you are. I wondered where you were. What are you doing out here?"

"Just thinking. You should maybe put some clothes on. You don't want to catch cold out here."

"I don't have any clothes to put on. This is my version of the Walk of Shame except that I can't walk home."

I laugh and put my arms around her. "I'll drive you home when you're ready."

"I don't want to leave yet." She follows my gaze toward the house. "What's on your mind?"

"Just.... everything. It's hard not to start planning our whole future when we don't even know if we have one."

She smiles at me in a way that tells me she understands. She doesn't mind me thinking about us having a future. "What do you think you might like to do with the rest of your life?"

"I honestly have no idea."

"You like building things. You must have enjoyed building that cabin."

"Yeah. I did." I frown at her. "How did you know?"

"Because you put so much time and attention and effort into it. You said you did it so you could have a decent place to live, but you could have built yourself a decent place to live without making it such a work of art."

My eyes pop. "A work of art! It's hardly that."

"Of course it is. That's what's so amazing about you. You don't even see it. You think this is all normal."

"It *is* normal. I've just been trying to rebuild my life. That's all I've done for the last six years."

"That's what I mean. It's normal to you. It isn't normal to anyone else." She waves again at the devastation that was once my dad's house. "What would you do with this if you rebuilt it?"

"I don't know. I've just been chipping away at the roof....and then I'd do the walls and floor. I didn't plan anything beyond that."

She leans against the truck and crosses her legs under the blanket. "Let me ask you something."

"Okay."

"Let your imagination run wild and imagine that, ten years from now, you're married with a bunch of kids running around."

I laugh. "What are you suggesting?"

"It could be with me or it could be with someone else. That's not important."

"Of course it's important."

She shoots me another grin and waves that away. "I'm not asking you that. I'm asking you what kind of house you would want to build for this hypothetical family you're going to have. What would you do with this place if you knew you were going to live the life of your dreams here?"

I frown at the rotten frames and the sagging floor. "I don't know. I guess I would build a bigger version of the cabin. I would do a lot of exposed beams, hardwood floors, big windows—all of that. I would want it to be a part of the surrounding natural beauty and also for the layout to give the people inside plenty of exposure to the natural beauty outside. I would want them to be able to see the surroundings all the time even when they were inside."

She watches my face while I talk. She doesn't say anything for so long that I start to feel self-conscious about what I just said.

I deflect it by changing the subject. "What about you? What do you think you'll do with the rest of your life?"

"I don't know." She turns back to the house and a shadow crosses her face. "I really don't know."

"So you asked me, but you don't ask yourself? How is that fair?"

She smiles, but that cloud comes back almost instantly.

"Do you think you want to keep doing media marketing?"

"If I did that, I would have to leave Oak Falls. I wouldn't be able to do it here."

"Why not? You could do it remotely."

She shrugs. She won't look at me.

"What about you ten years from now when you're married to the guy of your dreams with a pack of kids running around?" I ask. "What do you see yourself doing then?"

She scowls at the house and doesn't answer. She frowns even more dangerously—exactly the way she did when I first met her. All the same simmering resentment and hostility comes back, but she doesn't direct it at me.

I want to bring her back to the happiness of yesterday and last night, but maybe that isn't possible. Maybe showing me her scars didn't change the underlying problem of her life. Maybe I can't fix that for her no matter what I do.

I put my arm around her shoulders and steer her back toward the cabin. "Come on up to the house. I'll make you breakfast."

I take her back up there and up to the bedroom. I give her some sweatpants and an old hoodie to wear while I make breakfast.

I go down to the kitchen and put a batch of biscuits in the oven while I fry some bacon and make gravy for the biscuits. I brew some coffee and cut up some fruit when my phone rings.

I check the screen and see that it's my brother Elias. I answer it and his face appears on the screen. "What's up, man?"

"How ya doing?" he asks. "Did you get those documents I sent you?"

"No. What documents?"

"I emailed you last night. My colleague in the Neurology Department is doing a clinical trial on a new experimental amnesia treatment. I checked it out and ran it past a few other colleagues of mine. It looks really promising and the treatment is free for anyone who takes part in the study."

"What is it? What's the treatment?"

"It's a combination of drug therapy and micro-electrical stimulation of the affected cortex."

"You mean like electroshock therapy? No thanks, man."

"Come on!" he chides. "This method uses micro-electrodes implanted in the brain and it's already been through four preliminary trials with promising results. Isn't it at least worth trying?"

I turn off the stove and wander over to the living room. I sit down on the couch thinking it over. "So your buddy in the Neurology Department—is he there at UMass with you?"

"Yeah. I've worked with him since med school. He's a good guy. He wouldn't run a trial like this without all the protocols in place. I know him. He's straight up. He takes it seriously. His mother lost her memory in an accident when he was a kid. This study means a lot to him—like it does to us."

"I don't know. I don't really want to travel across the country for something that might not even work. I'm happy where I am."

His expression changes. "Look, man. You took a bullet for Luis and me when you stayed home to take care of Dad. You didn't have to do that and we're both grateful, but Dad's gone. You don't have to stay in Oak Falls. You're successful and you're living a functional life. You don't have to hide anymore. Alana and I have that rental behind our house. You could stay with us during the trial until you find your own place. We would love to have you and you could get to know the kids. Come on, man. You don't have to live alone. You can have a family."

I cringe. "It isn't like that."

"Of course it is." His voice breaks with emotion. "Don't you know what it would mean to all of us if you got your memory back? We would get *you* back. You don't know what we lost when we lost you."

"Yeah," I murmur. "I know."

"You don't know because you don't remember. It just breaks me up thinking about you living there alone in that shithole......"

"I don't live in a shithole." I try to keep my voice under control and fail. I can't lose my composure with this guy.

"You took care of Dad in a way that neither Luis nor I could. We'll never be able to repay you for that, but maybe we can be a family again. At least take a look at the documents and see what you think."

"Okay. I'll take a look."

He gulps and looks away from the screen. "We need you. I need you. It's even worse than if you died because you're still there. We never even got to grieve for you."

I can't answer. I don't even know what he's talking about. That's the worst part. I have no idea what he lost when I lost my memory. I don't have the first clue what might have been going on between me and my brothers before this happened. I'm not sure I want to know.

"All right, man," I tell him. "I'll take a look and then we'll see what we can do about the logistics."

His expression clears instantly. "Thanks, man. I can't wait to see you."

He hangs up and I let my phone fall into my lap. I gaze through the windows at the mountains outside. The view should relax me and make me happy the way it always does.

This is the first time that it doesn't make me happy. Everything about this place suddenly means something else—something I don't want it to mean.

I can't stay here. I stand up, and when I turn around, I cringe again when I see Jordan standing in the loft upstairs. She stares down at me and her lip trembles. She must have heard the whole conversation.

I turn away feeling sick to my stomach. "Breakfast is ready. I gotta go out for a while. I'll be back later."

I dive for the door and make it all the way out to my truck before she comes charging after me. "Wait, Rafe! Don't leave!"

"I have to. I need to get out of here. I need to think."

"Are you going to the overlook? Let me come with you. Don't go alone."

I freeze with my hand on the driver's door. I don't want to take her. I need to be alone.

"Let me help you," she breathes. "Let me be there for you. I want to. It doesn't have to mean anything. I won't lay any obligation on you. Just let me share.....whatever this is that you're going through. Please. I want to."

I pull open the door and get behind the wheel. I can't look at her, but I keep myself under control just long enough for her to get into the passenger seat.

I don't acknowledge her presence all the way to the overlook. I get out, walk out to my rock, sit down, and stare at the view thinking about everything.

She doesn't show up for a long, long time. She must have been sitting there alone and leaving me to my own devices.

I don't realize until she sits down next to me that I wanted her here all along. I thought I wanted to be alone, but now that she's here, she fills a void I didn't realize was there.

What if Elias is right about that, too? What if I don't know what I'm missing? I won't know if I don't at least try to get my memory back.

Do I even want a family like that? Would I want to have two brothers on opposite sides of the country? Would that be worth losing all this?

She moves her hand toward me, but she stops herself from touching me and lets her hand fall. "Do you want to talk about it?"

"No," I snap much more viciously than I mean to. I wince at my tone and try to soften it, but I don't succeed very well. "I don't think I can leave this place.....not even for you."

"I wouldn't want you to leave it for me. I wouldn't want to make you unhappy. This means too much to you."

"Does that mean we can't have a future? Does that mean you'll leave and I'll stay here?"

"I don't know. I don't know what's going to happen.....but I want to try. I want us to try to have a future. I understand if you don't, but it would be nice to think we could at least move it in that direction. I don't want to end it so soon just because you want to stay here and I....."

She breaks off. She doesn't say what she would do besides stay here.

That silence makes my stomach turn. How did one phone call shatter all my happiness and calm?

"What do you think you'll do about the treatment?" she asks. "Do you think you'll try it?"

"Who knows if it will even happen? I guess I could try it and then come back here. Then again, I might try it and get my memory back and realize I don't want to come back here. Maybe I'll be happy to stay in Boston and you can keep doing your marketing and everything will be perfect."

She can't fail to hear the cutting tone in my voice. I wish I wasn't like this. I would give anything to go back to being as happy as I was yesterday.

"I don't want you to do the treatment."

I snap around fast and stare at her. "What?!"

"I don't want you to do it. I don't want you to get your memory back. I don't want to run the risk that you'll turn back into the person you were before. I like you the way you are. I wouldn't want to lose that."

I can't stop gaping at her. She's talking like we're already a couple. She wouldn't say this if she wasn't serious about us.

She tears her gaze away. "I know I don't have any right to say that considering that we aren't even really together. Your family has much more of a claim on you than I do."

"But you don't even know if you want to stay here, either. You might decide that you want to leave and then there would be nothing between us."

She shrugs. "You're right."

I look back out at the view for a while. "I have to tell you something."

"Okay," she murmurs. "I'm listening."

I pull out my phone and tap on it a few times. I navigate to a certain webpage and hand her the phone. "My brothers and I belong to a real estate investment trust worth about $500 million."

"You said your portfolio was worth $20 million."

"That's my private portfolio. This is much bigger and it has about thirty other investors. My brothers and I have been talking about pulling out our stake and starting our own trust with the three of us as joint executive officers."

She frowns at my phone showing apartment buildings, skyscraper office towers, and several resorts on the page. "Why are you telling me this?"

"Because we would need to do a marketing campaign to recruit investors into our trust. We would need an ongoing marketing executive to handle our investor recruitment program and advertising going forward. We've been looking for the right person.....and I think I found her."

Her eyes flick up to my face. "Are you saying.... you want me to do this?"

"It would be totally remote. You could do it from anywhere."

"But if things didn't work out between us....."

I shrug. "That's a risk both you and I would have to take. If it didn't work out, you would have to find another job and we would have to find another marketing executive.....or you might decide that you wanted to lay off the marketing to concentrate on your family and your children.....regardless of who you have them with."

She blinks once as all of this sinks in. She looks down at my phone and then back up at me with some of her old burning fire. "I would have to think about that."

"Of course." I take the phone back from her. "Let's go back to my place and have some breakfast."

Chapter 17:
Jordan

I swish my forearms in a sink full of soapy water to wash the breakfast dishes. Rafe takes his phone over to the living room couch, collapses onto it, and raises his phone in front of his face. "All right. Let's see what this clinical trial is all about."

I flinch, but he doesn't see. I keep washing the dishes while he talks to himself. "This doctor running the trial certainly has his credentials. Elias was right about that. The dude won four awards for neurology and he's on the governing board at UMass School of Medicine."

He scrolls for a while and then calls to me over his shoulder. "What do you know? A few other researchers have been doing the same treatment protocol at Stanford with a seventy-three percent success rate. Maybe it actually works."

I still don't say anything. I can't think of a worse outcome than for Rafe to get his memory back. His brothers might want the boy Rafe was in high school, but I sure don't.

I finish rinsing the dishes, dry my hands, and wander over there. He's still scrolling through something while he reads.

"The trial isn't even scheduled until January of next year. Anything could happen between now and then." He raises his finger to tap the screen again. "I'll email Elias and tell him I've read the documents. He'll probably start booking my airline tickets and everything......"

I reach out and cover the phone with my hand. "Rafe.....I really don't want you to do this."

"But you said you weren't even sure if we were together. You could decide that we aren't and that you don't want to stay in Oak Falls and that I'm not someone you want to have a future with at all. How can I make a decision like this just because you don't want me to? You have to give me something more to go on."

I inhale a deep breath. He's right. I need to give him more of a reason to consider my opinion. "I......I love you."

He freezes and stares at me with his mouth open.

"I don't know what's going to happen, but I want to at least try to have a future with you. I can't do that if you do this trial."

"But...." He gulps pulling himself back to reality. "Why? If it works and I get my memory back, I wouldn't forget everything that happened between us. I would remember all of that plus whatever happened before I lost it. I would still feel the same way about you."

"Which is what? How exactly do you feel about me?"

He opens his mouth again, but no sound comes out.

I ease over to the couch to sit next to him. I take the phone out of his hand and put it on the coffee table. It's decision time. We can't go any further without laying all our cards on the table and that means I need to be totally honest with him. He deserves that.

"I told you at the overlook that I didn't want you to do this trial because I didn't want your personality to go back to the way it was in high school."

He nods. "I can understand that."

"I love you and I don't want anything to change you.....but that's not the real reason I don't want you to do this trial. There's another reason." He stares at me with such a stunned expression that I have no choice but to go on. "You're the person who saved my life. You're the person who pulled me from the car when Raleigh drove off the overlook. I think.....I think maybe that might be the reason you got hurt—because you were helping me."

He blinks at me a few times and then turns to stare straight in front of him. He doesn't say anything at first.

I take his hand, but he hardly responds. "You were the person who saved me before you lost your memory. I know that now, but I still don't want you to change back into that person. Last night.....you made my scars mean something different. I've always been ashamed of them, but now they mean you. They're the evidence that you saved my life and I love you for that. I don't want anything to change between us. I would gladly stay here with you if it means we can be together."

I squeeze his hand and he startles out of his trance. He looks down at me and his eyes glisten with emotion. "You are so beautiful. Any man would be lucky to have you."

I have to kiss him. "I don't want any other man. I want you. I don't want any other man to look at my scars—ever. I want that to be all for you."

I sink into kissing him again and his arms close around me. His arms and hands and lips tell me that he wants that, too. He wants me all to himself and I want him to have that.

He pulls me onto his lap, but his kiss means something new and special. It changes every time I kiss him, every time we talk, every time we get closer. That kiss becomes more sensual, more emotional, and more excruciatingly meaningful.

I don't want it to end. I want to give him something so much deeper and more unique to him.

He pulls my legs around his waist, but when he draws me down on his swelling bulge, I can't go through with it.

I tip him sideways and lay him down on his back on the couch. I slide my hands under his shirt, push it up, and kiss his chest and stomach the way I did last night in his truck.

He gasps and tenses when my mouth touches his sides, but he doesn't stop me from pulling his shirt off. I revel in the glorious ecstasy of adoring his skin with my mouth and teeth and tongue.

He follows my movements with his hands, but he doesn't stop me. I want to worship him and smother him with all the love and lust in my heart. I want to take him to Heaven the way he keeps taking me there. I want to give him some small fraction of the pleasure and happiness that he gives me.

I pull his sweatpants down and his rigid member falls into my mouth. Now I get to suck him as long and as deeply as I want to. We aren't in the cab of his truck. We're in his house, and if this works out between us, it will be our house.

He lifts his hips for me to slide his pants off. His beautiful naked body spreads before me the way he asked me to spread myself before him last night. He arches his back and groans in agony when I suck him. His chest shudders and his breath catches every time he breathes.

I love seeing him like this. I love seeing him in ecstasy at my touch. I love feeling him throb in my mouth and knowing that I'm the one giving him this pleasure.

His fingers clamp on my shoulders and his arms strain. I can't tell if he's pulling me in or pushing me off. Every muscle tightens to the breaking point and his abs tremble with tortured breath.

He turns his head into the couch whining with pleasure. I can't stop running my hands over his body. Every crevice and furrow electrifies me. This is mine. This is all mine. I don't want anyone else touching him ever again. I want him all to myself.

"God, baby......oh, my God....."

I love hearing him talk like that. I could suck him to completion like this, but I want to see him when I take him there. I want to look into his eyes and for both of us to know that we're going there together.

I climb up his body slipping out of my clothes. He groans again when my lips slither off the end of his shaft. I sneak up his body kissing his thighs, his stomach, his chest, and his neck before I reach his mouth.

He kisses me back and gasps again when I sink down on his rigid spike. It buries in my deepest being and I sit up straight where we can both see each other.

His eyes lock on mine as I start to rock. He grabs my hips to join his rhythm with mine and his eyes float in a haze of magical pleasure. "Baby.... you are so beautiful......"

His hands follow my curves as I move. He cups my breasts and then slides back down to corkscrew into me from below. I ride the waves of rapture flowing into me from his body. I hover in the clouds of heavenly bliss feasting my heart and soul on his eyes and face and skin.

He's so beautiful to me—not because of what he looks like on the outside, but for the person he is on the inside. He's intelligent and interesting and insightful and understanding and intriguing and creative and helpful and compassionate.

All of those things make him beautiful on the inside. They bleed through to the exterior and make him beautiful on the outside, too. I've never seen anyone more beautiful than he looks right now when I gaze down at his face.

His insatiable rhythm floods me with pleasure and fulfillment. I don't want this to end. Even his hands touching my scars fill me with so much love and desire that I can't stand it.

I arch my back letting him see my whole body, but as the wave carries me higher toward my inevitable climax, I can't stay away from him.

I collapse over him and all my dreams come true when I kiss him. Our lips join in a seamless whole with our bodies moving in a steady, driving tide that can only end one way.

His arms surround me and I melt on his iron frame as his thrusts propel me to the stratospheric heights of bliss.

Chapter 18: Rafe

I pull my truck into the driveway at Jordan's parents' house and she makes a face. "Anita's still here. I wonder why."

"I'll just stay here while you go inside and get your stuff."

"No, come inside with me. It's time we dealt with this once and for all and I don't want you lurking out here like a shameful secret."

"I don't know if I want to hear a grown woman get spanked for bad behavior. That's an experience I'd rather not carry with me for the rest of my life."

She laughs. "Come inside. This is my house, not hers, and you're my guest."

"Do I have to?"

"Yes, you have to. You can sit in the living room and talk to my dad if you want to."

I grumble under my breath, but she only beams at me. She takes my hand and tows me out of the truck, up the steps, and inside.

She calls, "Hi, Dad!" into the living room.

Her father doesn't even look up from his paper. "How ya doing, sweetie?"

"I'm good. I'm just picking up a few things and then I'm going back over to Rafe's house."

He still doesn't react. "Okay, sweetie. Tell your mom if you won't be home for dinner."

Jordan goes to the end of the hall and throws open a different door. It leads into the kitchen where her mother sits across the counter from Anita. "I won't be home for dinner, Mom," Jordan announces. "I'm going over to Rafe's house for a while."

"How long is a while?" her mother asks.

"I don't know. I'll let you know."

Anita looks past Jordan's shoulder and curls her lip, but she stops short of saying anything, thank goodness.

Jordan shuts the door in her face, grimaces at me, and turns toward the stairs. "I'll go get my stuff. You can go in the living room if you want or you can come with me."

"Are you sure he won't mind?"

"Of course he won't." She kisses me on the cheek. "I'll be right back and then we can get out of here."

She dashes upstairs and I wander into the living room. Her father glances up at me, smiles, and then bends over his paper. "How ya doing, son?"

"I'm good, Sir. Thanks for asking."

"It looks like Max Wilkins is challenging Holden Keller for County Commissioner. That should be an interesting race."

I don't reply. I meander to the mantle shelf and check out pictures of Jordan as a girl along with her parents and a few other people who are probably her siblings. It must be nice to have a home with pictures of your past that mean something to you.

"I hear your brother Elias is a big-shot doctor at UMass now," Isaac goes on without looking up from his paper. "Did you know he wanted to be a cop when he was in high school? He did a few ride-alongs with the department before he left for college."

"Yeah. He started doing Criminal Justice and switched to pre-med in his third year of college." I don't tell him why Elias went into medicine. I don't tell Isaac that Elias decided to become a doctor because of what happened to me. Isaac doesn't need to know that.

He shoots me another grin over his paper. Something in his eyes tells me he knows more than he's letting on, but he doesn't say anything.

I start reading the book spines on the shelf when loud voices echo through the house. They come from upstairs, and as soon as I hear them, I know more than I ever wanted to about why everyone is so upset.

"Are you out of your tree?" Anita snarls. "Why don't you just throw your whole life away while you're at it?"

"Will you mind your own business?" Jordan fires back. "I told you last week to keep your comments about my love life to yourself. You got all upset and asked if we were still friends. It sure looks from where I'm standing like you're working overtime to flush what little is left of our friendship down the crapper."

"I'm saying this because I'm your friend and I care about you," Anita counters. "He's a loser and a criminal. You don't know what you're getting into."

"You don't know what the hell you're talking about!" Jordan snaps. "You really need to learn to keep your mouth shut."

Anita gasps. "You take that back!"

"At least hear Anita out," Jordan's mother interjects. "Don't you think it would be better to consider all the facts before you go running off with a guy you barely know?"

"I know all I need to know." Jordan's rapid footsteps cross the upstairs getting closer to the stairs.

"Going out with him or even making out with him is one thing," Anita adds. "You can't go over to his house."

"Watch me," Jordan snarls.

"We're just worried about you," her mother quavers. "You could vanish into the mountains and we might never see you again."

I glance over at Isaac to find him staring at me, but his eyes look sad and very understanding. He doesn't look angry or suspicious that his daughter is coming back to my house indefinitely.

Her words come back to me. Does he know about me losing my memory?

Jordan's heels pound on the stairs as she comes running down from her room. She's wearing her usual casual jeans and denim jacket and she carries a backpack over her shoulder.

"You have a phone and I have a phone, Mom," she calls over her shoulder. "You can call me every day if you're that worried."

"But.... how will we know if anything happens?" her mother asks.

"Nothing will happen except that I might not want to have anything to do with any of you if you don't pull your heads out of your asses."

Her mother practically screams. "Jordan! How could you?"

Jordan pauses just long enough to hold up her hand. "Don't talk to me, Mom. Don't talk to me at all about anything ever again." She shoots Anita a hateful glare and darts into the living room.

Jordan bends over and kisses her father on the cheek. "I love you, Dad. I'll see you soon."

"Okay. See you soon, sweetie."

"Come on, Rafe," Jordan mutters. "Let's get the hell out of here."

Her mother and Anita hustle into the living room and plant themselves across the threshold to box us in. "Aren't you even going to talk to her, Mr. Cruz?" Anita asks. "Aren't you at least going to try to stop her?"

"Why would I do that?" he asks. "She's a grown woman. She can decide who she goes out with."

"Thank you, Dad," Jordan turns back to the other two. "You hear that? At least not everyone in this house has gone completely around the bend."

"Do you remember what he did to Suzie Augustine?" Anita interjects. "And that's nothing compared to what Sheila Watson said he did to her."

"What did she say?" Isaac asks.

"What difference does it make what she said?" Jordan counters. "If it wasn't important enough for the Police Department to press charges, then it's just hearsay and we can all ignore it."

"You're right." Isaac shakes out his paper, turns a page, and goes back to scanning the columns. "Call us if you need anything, sweetheart."

I shrink when I see the expressions on Anita's and Jordan's mother's faces. They don't move and they don't look like they're in any danger of letting me out of this room anytime soon.

"Get out of the way, Mom," Jordan hisses. "You and Anita have said all you have to say. Rafe and I are leaving."

"Not until you explain why you want to throw your life away with such a....a scumbag."

"Rafe is not a scumbag," Jordan returns. "You don't know what you're talking about. You and Anita are too stupid to know your asses from your elbows. You wouldn't open your mouths about Rafe if you didn't have your heads buried so far underground that you don't even know it."

"Why can't you explain it to us?" her mother asks. "We watched him grow up in this town and Anita went to high school with him the same way you did. What do you know that we don't?"

Jordan hesitates, but she doesn't look at me. She looks down at her father and he looks up at her with the same warm, understanding expression. She was dead right about him. He knows a whole hell of a lot more than he lets on.

Jordan takes a deep breath and faces her mother and best friend. "Rafe is the one who pulled me out of the car when Raleigh drove off the Desolation Heights overlook. Rafe is the one who dragged me up to the road and saved my life."

Anita's jaw drops and Jordan's mother gasps. She looks back and forth between me and Jordan. "Are you sure? How do you know? No one ever found out who pulled you from the car."

"Someone found out. Dad was the cop who found Rafe after the wreck. He found him on Desolation Heights Road less than thirty-six hours after the crash and he drove Rafe to the hospital."

Jordan's mother looks down at her husband, but the woman doesn't say anything. There's nothing to say. So Isaac knew all along. He knew more than just the fact that I lost my memory. He knew how and where and why I lost my memory.

Jordan makes sure she gets the right reaction from her mother. Anita stands there with her mouth open. She doesn't say a word. Good. I hope she never says a word to me ever again.

Jordan slips her hand into mine and squeezes. "Let's get out of here."

"Hold on a second," I tell her. "Not yet."

She frowns until I turn to her father. "Excuse me, Sir, but I was hoping I could get your permission to marry your daughter."

"What?!" Jordan shrieks.

I keep my attention on Isaac. I was worried about asking, but now I'm certain. "If she'll have me, of course."

He smiles up at me and he looks genuinely happy for the first time. "If Jordan wants to marry you, son, we would be delighted to welcome you into our family. No man could ask for a better son-in-law." He stands up and extends his hand to me. "I'm sure you'll make her very happy."

"Isaac!" Jordan's mother gasps.

Isaac glances at her and Anita and then smiles at me. "Go on home, son. I'll deal with these two."

"Thank you, Sir."

I take Jordan's hand and I have to shoulder my way out of the room. Anita still doesn't move, but Jordan's mother recoils from me with another horrified gasp. That leaves me plenty of room to get Jordan out of the house.

Chapter 19: Jordan

I collapse against the side of Rafe's truck and cover my eyes. "I'm so sorry! I'm so sorry you had to listen to that."

"It's okay," he murmurs. "It was worth it."

My head shoots up. "Worth it! How can you even say that?"

"They know now. They know about me....and I got your dad's permission to marry you."

I freeze staring at him. "You're serious."

"Of course I'm serious. Marry me. You know I can make you happy. We'll work out the details of where we're going to live and why later on. You can work for our real estate trust....or not, depending on what you decide. It doesn't matter as long as we're together."

I stare at him as this latest lightning bolt blows my mind. Marry him?

He wraps his arms around me and kisses me on the forehead. "Thank you. That was incredible. No one has ever done anything like that for me. I want to marry you. I was worried about asking your dad, but now I know that everything's okay."

"What are we going to do about Mom and Anita? If we stay in this town, we'll have to keep dealing with them and everyone else who thinks you're a scumbag."

He bursts out laughing. "It would almost be worth staying in this town after what you just did. I would love for anyone to come up to me on the street and call me a scumbag after that."

I can't look at him. I hide in his arms feeling small. I wish I could erase all their hateful remarks from my memory. I almost wish we could leave town and start over somewhere else.

He kisses me again and pushes me away. "Let's go home. This is nothing. Your dad will deal with them and then we won't have any more problems with them."

"Are you sure?"

"I'm sure. I trust him. Come on. Take your backpack and get in your car. You can follow me back to the cabin and then we'll talk about what happens next."

"What happens next?"

He smiles at me. "I don't know, but I'm excited to find out."

He gives me one last kiss and propels me toward my car. He climbs into the truck and idles while I buckle my seat belt and start the motor.

I cast a backward glance toward my parents' house before I pull away. I don't want to know what's going on in there between my dad, my mom, and Anita, but Rafe is right. I trust my dad to handle things.

He kept Rafe's secret for six years. He'll make my mom and Anita understand that they need to keep this confidential and also that they need to change their attitude toward Rafe. This is long overdue.

Rafe eases his truck onto the road and I pull out behind him. We have our whole future in front of us. My spirits lift as I put more distance between myself and my parents' house. I don't need to dwell on the past anymore. The future is way too interesting and holds too many possibilities.

The sun breaks through the treetops as I turn the corner. Things are looking up. Now I just have to stop these butterflies in my stomach from getting the better of me every time I think about marrying Rafe. Are we really doing this?

Just a few weeks ago, I thought I would never find anyone, never have a family, and never find where I belonged or what I wanted to do.

Am I really going to marry Rafe? Are we going to start a family on the same mountain where I grew up? It sounds like a dream come true. I don't want to believe it, but it's really happening.

Unstoppable excitement and happiness overcome me. I haven't felt this happy since I made the decision to go out with Rafe. This is going to be great. All my dreams are coming true in the best possible way. This is going to be even better than my dream come true.

Rafe drives at a leisurely pace so I have no problem staying behind him. All the things we need to discuss crowd my mind, but I can put them aside. We'll work it out. I'm certain of it.

He turns off Saddle Mountain Road heading for his place. The sun swivels around to the western side of the mountain. Another day has passed—the first day of the rest of our lives.

I rest my elbow on the windowsill feeling...good. I haven't felt this good since before the car accident. If things keep going this way, I could keep feeling this good forever. What would my life look like then?

Rafe's truck swings around another curve. He's still driving at the same relaxed pace when, without warning, a dark blue BMW rockets around the next curve. It crosses the center line, tries to correct, and fails before it skids out of control and swipes Rafe's truck.

The pickup screeches sideways, smashes through the guard rail, and cartwheels into the air before the BMW comes careening straight for me.

I yank the wheel just in time to avoid a full head-on collision. The BMW fishtails out of the way and vanishes as my car peels into a skid, hits something, and vaults skyward.

I crush the wheel in a death grip and hunch my shoulders as the car tumbles out of control. It somersaults over and over from one side to the other. The windshield smashes in and the roof caves. It bangs into my head and the car turns another revolution before it slams down hard on its roof.

Dead silence falls over the car and I dare to look around. I'm hanging upside down in my seatbelt with trees, dirt, and branches covering the front windshield.

I fight to breathe, but at least I'm not hurt. Both passenger windows have been smashed out. I can get out of the car if I can just take my seatbelt off.

I unclip it and fall on my head with a yell before I scramble out onto solid ground. I crouch there panting on all fours trying to switch my brain into gear. I'm okay. I'm alive and unhurt.... but what about Rafe?

I dare to look around and my hair stands on end when I see the BMW parked by the side of the road. Holden Keller stands there gaping in horror at my car.

Rage boils in my blood when I see the scratch marks running the length of his car. He drove me and Rafe off the road. Where is Rafe?

I stagger to my feet and advance back toward the road. Holden stands there in shock staring at me....and then his eyes swivel to his left.

I follow his gaze and see Rafe's pickup flattened against a tree. He lies crumpled on the ground outside the smashed windshield. Cuts, gashes, and bruising disfigure his face. He must have flown through the windshield.

I lurch up to the road. "Help us, Holden!" I yell. "Call 911!"

He doesn't move except to stare from one car to the next. Every minute that he doesn't do anything infuriates me even more. "Do something, Holden!" I bellow. "Don't just stand there!"

I step over the guardrail and grab him by the jacket. I shake him hard and then, when he still doesn't react, I slap him. "You bastard! You did this! You could have killed us both!"

Those words send a jet of ice-cold terror to my heart. What if Rafe is dead? He can't be. He just can't be.

"Call 911!" I yell again, but when Holden still doesn't do anything, I attack him patting down his clothes. "Give me your phone!"

He snaps out of his trance, tears away from me, and stumbles backward toward his car. "Holden!" I roar. "Holden! Don't you dare run off!"

He doesn't listen, and when I try to follow him, my head swims. Maybe I'm not as unhurt as I thought.

Holden rips open the driver's door, dives into the seat, and screeches away down the mountain taking his phone with him.

I have to help Rafe and I don't have time to go find my own phone. I jump over the guard rail and blunder down to the truck.

I whimper in anguish when I turn him over and see how bad his injuries are. His face is a mass of cuts and pulpy bruising, but at least he's still breathing.

I claw at his pockets until I find his phone. I dial 911 with shaking hands. "911 emergency dispatch," the operator clips. "Please state the nature of your emergency."

"There's......there's been a car accident. Someone.... ran us off the road. My....my...." What am I supposed to say? Is Rafe my boyfriend or.... "My fiancé...he's hurt....we need an ambulance."

"I'm tracking your location now, Ma'am," the operator tells me. "Are you at the 51-mile marker, Blacktop Mountain Road, Oak Falls?"

"Uh.... yeah." I check the mile marker nearest me. "My fiancé....his car is down in a gully. I'll try to get him out."

"I'm dispatching ambulance, fire, and Police now, Ma'am. Stay on the line until the emergency crews arrive."

I press the phone to my ear trying to control my panic. Rafe has to be okay. He has to.

Just then, he moans and coughs. He lurches onto his side. "Jordan...."

"I'm here!" I tell him. "I'm here! The ambulance is on its way. Hang on!"

He rolls onto his hands and knees and retches a mouthful of bloody saliva onto the ground. "Jordan...."

"I'm here." I touch his shoulder. "Just take it easy. The ambulance is on its way. I'm going up to the road to flag them down."

"Don't.... leave me.... alone...." He tries to stand up. "Don't.... leave me...."

I can't stand listening to that. "Come on. I'll take you with me."

I'm too relieved that he's conscious to argue. I get under his arm and haul him to his feet. He stumbles and his weight sags against me, but I don't care. I have to get him to safety. I have to make sure he's all right. At least he knows who I am. He didn't lose his memory again.

I force myself up the slope to the road. He crashes onto his knees more than once and I practically break my spine picking him up. I haul him to the guard rail where he collapses. I can't lift him over it, but just as I'm wondering if I should sit him up or lie him down, I hear sirens in the distance.

A fire truck comes screaming around the bend followed by an ambulance. I jump up waving my arms and they skid in next to me. I wave the firefighters and paramedics toward Rafe. They surround him and I get pushed aside.

"Jordan!" he hollers. "Jordan.... don't leave me.....!"

"I'm right here!" I try to reach him. "I'm here! I'm with you!"

He flounders to get away from the medics. Some of the firefighters try to lead me away. "Let me go with him!" I scream. "Let me go with him!"

They finally decide that we're both better off if we stay together. I climb into the ambulance where the medics are strapping Rafe to their stretcher. "Jordan...!" he yells through ruined lips. "Where are you? I can't see you!"

"I'm here!" I grab his hand. "I'm right here! I'm not going anywhere!"

He relaxes back on the stretcher and tries to look around, but his eyes are so swollen that I can't even see them anymore. I hang onto his hand and he crushes my fingers in a death grip as the ambulance peels away and takes off down the mountain.

Chapter 20: Rafe

I flounder back to consciousness and try to look around, but everything's pitch dark. "Jordan!" I shriek. "Jordan, where are you?"

Her hand closes around mine. "I'm here. I'm right here. You're safe. You don't have to worry anymore."

"Why can't I see anything? Why is it so dark?"

"Your eyes are still covered in bandages. Your whole head is bandaged. You went through the windshield and you've been in and out of surgery a bunch of times, but you're okay."

I turn toward her voice. Her even, steady tone calms me as much as I can be calmed under the circumstances. "I need to see you."

Her satin lips touch my hand. "I have to tell you something. Your eyes got damaged in the accident. There's a chance you might be blind."

"No!" I groan.

She kisses my hands again and I feel her touching my body. "It's all right. We'll still be together."

"Why did this have to happen? Everything was going so well."

"Everything is still going well. We're still together and we're going to stay together. Nothing can stop that."

She puts her arms around me and hugs me. She kisses the side of my head, but her lips don't reach my skin. Now I feel the bandages. Everything gets in the way of me being with her.

"That bastard Holden!" I snarl.

She chuckles. "He's in Police custody. He won't be running for office anytime soon—if ever."

"How can you laugh about this? This is a disaster."

"I'm happy," she murmurs in my ear. "I'm happy because you're awake after more than a week in a coma and I'm happy that we're together. Being with you is the best thing that ever happened to me. Holden can't change that. No disaster can take you away from me."

She kisses me again and I feel her climb onto my bed. She puts her arms around me and sinks down on the bed next to me. I collapse into her embrace. I want so badly to see her and kiss her and be with her the way we were before, but this will have to be good enough for now.

"Your brother Elias flew in right after the accident. He's been running rings around the doctors ever since."

I snort. "Does he still want me to do the clinical trial?"

"He didn't mention it. The doctors planned to come in today and take the bandages off your eyes. You should find out in a few hours if you can see."

"Great," I grumble.

She kisses me again and sighs in what I can only imagine is an ecstasy of relief. I should be grateful. I still have her and I still have my memory. I can live with being blind as long as I have those two things.

Just then, I hear some noise in the distance and Jordan stiffens. "Here comes the medical team."

A door opens somewhere and I hear a bunch of people come in. A strong male hand grips my arm. "Hey, man!" It's Elias. "You're awake just in time! The doctors are going to take your bandages off so we'll finally know where we're at with your eyes."

"Thanks for coming, man," I tell him. "I really appreciate it."

"Forget it. You think I'd let my baby brother go through this by himself?"

I don't mention Jordan. Is it possible that Jordan and Elias have been in the same hospital and Elias doesn't know yet that Jordan and I are together?

Now isn't the time to break the news. A woman comes toward me and touches my shoulder. "I'm going to start cutting the bandages, Rafe. You might feel some pinching when the tape comes off."

I try to relax on the pillows as more people move in. They wedge their scissors under the bandages and start cutting. I keep a tight hold on Jordan's hand. I don't want to lose her in the darkness, especially if the darkness turns out to be permanent.

Some of the tape gets stuck in my hair and I flinch when the medical team pulls the bandages away from my face. I feel how slashed and battered my face and head are. I'm a mess, but at least I'll be able to feel when Jordan kisses me. That's a small mercy.

The medical team unwinds acres and acres of fabric from my head and then the woman doctor says, "This is it. I'm going to unwrap the covering on your eyes and remove the gauze. You'll be able to open your eyes and you can tell us what you see."

She peels the gauze away and then lifts two cloth squares from my eyelids. Nothing happens at first. I try to see, but my eyelids are so stuck together that I can't pry them apart.

"Here," the woman says. "Let me clean some of the dried blood off your eyelids."

I have to fight the urge to yell when she presses a cold swab to my eyes. They hurt like hell, but a second later, one of my eyelids comes unstuck.

The very first thing I see is Jordan's beautiful face right in front of me. Her eyes bore into my soul exactly the way I remember. I burst out laughing in pure, blessed relief that I can see her. "Hey, baby!"

She beams at me and tears well up in her eyes. "Hey. It's so good to see you."

I can't stop laughing, I'm so fucking happy to see her. I barely notice when the doctor lady swabs my other eye and that opens, too. I can see! I can see Jordan.

More heads move into my line of sight. They're all strangers except for Elias. His features twists with emotion. I should pay more attention to him, but I can't stop looking at Jordan. I don't give a shit about anybody else. I want to cry, she looks so damn beautiful.

The doctor lady starts rattling on about vision tests and CT scans and a whole lot of other stuff I don't care about. Elias runs interference for me until the medical team leaves. I wish he'd leave, too. I want to be alone with Jordan.

He keeps hanging around, though. He ushers the medical team out of the room before he comes over to me and grips my arm. "It's such a relief that you can see. You've been through enough for one lifetime."

I force myself to look up at him. "I'm sorry, man, but I'm not going to do the clinical trial."

"Why not? This is your chance to get it all back. I thought we discussed this."

"We did, but I'm not doing it. I met someone......It's complicated, but I'm not doing it. This is just the way it is."

His eyes skip sideways to Jordan. She still holds my hand and never once moves away from my side.

Elias scowls at her and then at me before he shrugs. "I guess I can understand that."

"I know all I need to know about the past. You and me and Luis....this is just the way it is now....and who knows? Maybe it would be like this anyway with you two moving away and me staying in Oak Falls."

He cracks a sudden grin. "I doubt that. You never would have made millions playing the stock market if you never got hit over the head."

I laugh. "You're right, so maybe something good came out of it after all."

Elias looks over at Jordan again. How much does he know? Did she tell him about how I got hurt?

He finally smiles at me. "All right, man. I can live with that."

"Thanks."

He shuffles his feet and finally jerks his thumb over his shoulder. "I'll get out of your hair. Let me know if you need anything, okay?"

"Okay. You'll be the first person I call."

I don't tell him that I'll call Jordan first, but that's okay, too. I doubt I'll have to call her because she is never leaving my side again as long as she lives.

He bends down and hugs me before he takes himself off somewhere. I can finally relax when the door swings shut behind him.

I turn to Jordan, sink back on my pillows with a heavy sigh, and feast my eyes on her face. My God, she's a sight for sore eyes—literally.

She smiles at me with tears brimming in her eyes and she kisses my hand. "I love you."

"You are so beautiful, baby," I croak. "You are the most beautiful woman in the world."

"You're beautiful, too." Her magical hands come to my face. I feel all the cuts and stitches crisscrossing my head all over, but she beams at me like I really am the most attractive man on the planet. "You have never been more beautiful to me than you are right now."

"Baby?" I can't speak above a whisper.

"Yes, my love?"

"Will you marry me?"

"Yes, darling." She bends down and kisses me on the forehead. It's the only part of my head that isn't cut to ribbons. "I would love to marry you."

"You won't turn your back on me because my face is covered in scars?"

She bursts into a huge grin and her tears streak down her face. "Of course not. You're intelligent and interesting and insightful and understanding and intriguing and creative and helpful and compassionate. Why should I care about a few scars?"

I gulp down rising emotion. I want so badly to kiss her right now, but my lips barely move when I speak. I don't want to get blood on her or to damage myself by overdoing it.

She doesn't seem to care. She kisses my forehead again and stretches out on the bed at my side. She nuzzles her head into the corner of my shoulder and wraps her arms around me. "Everything is going to be wonderful. You'll see."

"Did you tell Elias about me pulling you from that car?"

"No. I didn't tell him anything."

I rest my head against hers and don't reply. No one needs to know. We know and that's enough. I'll get out of this hospital one of these days and then our whole beautiful future will unfold exactly the way we want it to. I'll make certain of it.

The End.

If you enjoyed this book, please consider leaving a review. You can also support me on Patreon at www.patreon.com/InvisiblePublishing.

Sign Up Once--Get all A.E. Moran's free books including brand new releases

When Doctor Lily Rice moves into a small mountain town to live in isolation away from the world, she sets off a chain of events no one could predict. Her arrival throws town doctor Parker Davis into turmoil. Is Lily trying to steal his patients and drive him out of practice.....or is there something much more sinister at work here?

The two get thrown together by circumstance and fate, only for secrets from both their pasts to threaten everything they've worked to build. Can two broken strangers find happiness through devastation before disaster tears them apart?

Sign up at www.authoraemoran.com to read it for free.

About AE Moran

A.E Moran is the contemporary romance pen name for Theo Mann.

I write 70 books per year—and yes, before you ask, all these books are my original creative work. Nothing written under my name is AI-generated or ghostwritten because I write better than AI and any ghostwriter out there.

People don't read fiction for entertainment or to escape from reality. People read fiction to see their humanity reflected in another person's character and story.

This is my promise to you. When you read my books, you'll see your own humanity reflected in the characters and stories. I take this commitment to my readers very seriously. My books are an intimate form of communication between us. I would never disrespect my readers by turning that over to a machine or another writer. This is my bond between me and you as my reader.

I write 20,000 words per day as my daily work output. If anyone with a public platform would like to challenge me to prove this in a controlled environment, feel free to contact me on this website's contact page. How do I do write so much? Find out more on my blog, *Crimes Against Fiction* at www.theomann.com.

I worked as a professional ghostwriter for fifteen years. Now I'm going for the Guinness World Record by writing 700 books over the next ten years and 1400 books over the next twenty years, all originally written by me.

See my website for the full book list. I'm also the author of *Proof for the Existence of God* and the *Crimes Against Fiction* blog.

You can find out more at www.theomann.com or at www.author aemoran.com.

Also by AE Moran (so far)